'You want  mistress?'

Sam could barely take in what he was saying, though she could feel the hollowness inside her filling with pain. His *mistress*. How cold and unloving he made it sound—a union purely for sex, with no love or emotional bonding shared between them. There were no words from him to reassure her that, even if his position meant that he did not want to marry her, at least he cared enough to understand how important it was to her to know that he felt love for her.

'It seems a logical solution to a situation which we both know is becoming untenable.'

She ought to turn him down and walk—no, run away from him, just as far as she could. If only for the sake of her own pride. But how would she feel once she had done that? How would she feel back home in England, knowing she could have been with him? Would her pride sustain her then, when she was lying awake at night hungering for him?

ARABIAN NIGHTS

Spent at the Sheikh's pleasure...
by
Penny Jordan

The Sheikh's Virgin Bride
One Night with the Sheikh
Possessed by the Sheikh
Prince of the Desert
Taken by the Sheikh
The Sheikh's Blackmailed Mistress

Welcome to the exotic lands of Zuran and Dhurahn,
beautiful, sand-swept places where sheikhs rule
and anything is possible...
Experience nights of passion under a desert moon!

THE SHEIKH'S BLACKMAILED MISTRESS

BY
PENNY JORDAN

MILLS & BOON
Pure reading pleasure

All the characters in this book have no existence outside the imagination of the author, and have no relation whatsoever to anyone bearing the same name or names. They are not even distantly inspired by any individual known or unknown to the author, and all the incidents are pure invention.

First published in Great Britain 2008
Harlequin Mills & Boon Limited,
Eton House, 18-24 Paradise Road, Richmond, Surrey TW9 1SR

© Penny Jordan 2008

ISBN: 978 0 263 86432 8

Set in Times Roman 10½ on 13 pt
01-0608-49070

Printed and bound in Spain
by Litografia Rosés, S.A., Barcelona

Penny Jordan has been writing for more than twenty years and has an outstanding record: over 170 novels published, including the phenomenally successful A PERFECT FAMILY, TO LOVE, HONOUR AND BETRAY, THE PERFECT SINNER and POWER PLAY, which hit the *Sunday Times* and *New York Times* bestseller lists. Penny Jordan was born in Preston, Lancashire, and now lives in rural Cheshire.

Recent titles by the same author:

TAKEN BY THE SHEIKH

The Royal House of Niroli:

THE FUTURE KING'S PREGNANT MISTRESS
A ROYAL BRIDE AT THE SHEIKH'S COMMAND

PROLOGUE

'OHHHH, NO!'

Her anxious warning protest had come too late, and now she was pressed hard against the very male body of the robed man who had been turning the corner at the same time from the opposite direction.

Her startled cry and the clear visual imprinting her eyes had relayed to her brain—of a tall, broad-shouldered and very arrogant-looking handsome male, with the most extraordinarily green eyes she had ever seen—was all there'd been time for before that image had been blanked out by her abrupt and far too intimate contact—visually and physically—with his body.

Now, with her face virtually buried against his shoulder, her senses were being assaulted by that intimacy in every sensory way that there was. She could feel the heat of his body, and smell its personal slightly musky male scent, mingled with the cool sharpness of the cologne he was wearing. She could feel, too, the heavy thud of his heart beating out a demand that called to her own heartbeat to follow it. Lean, strong fingers gripped her arm, bare flesh to bare flesh setting a panicky, firework-intense burst of lava-hot sensation spilling through her own body.

The manner in which they had collided had brought her up against him in such a way that she now realised she was leaning against one of his thighs, her own having somehow softened and parted to admit its muscular male presence. The lava flow changed from a rolling surge of heat into an explosion of female arousal that wrenched any kind of control over her body from her and claimed it for itself. Quivers of female recognition at his maleness were softening her flesh into his. Breathing was becoming a dangerously erotic hazard that leached her small soft moan of longing into the once sterile silence of the corridor.

She mustn't do this. She mustn't raise her head from the muscle-padded warmth of his shoulder to look up into his face. She mustn't let her desire-dazed gaze dwell yearningly on his mouth. She mustn't quiver and then sigh, and then place her hand on his chest, whilst lifting her gaze reluctantly from his mouth to his eyes, so that her own could whisper to him how much she ached to trace the sensuality of that full lower lip set beneath its sharply cut partner with her fingertip, or better still with her tongue-tip, caressing it into a reciprocal hunger for the kiss she now wanted so badly.

No, she must not do any of those things—but she was doing them, and he was looking back at her as though he wanted exactly what she wanted, and for all the same reasons.

The air in the corridor hadn't changed, but she still shivered and trembled and then moaned as he lowered his head to hers, his free hand sliding into the untidy tangle of her honey-streaked curls.

She could feel the warmth of his breath against her skin—feel it and taste it, with its erotic mix of promised delights. Longingly she watched the slow descent of his mouth towards her own, savouring each millimetre of movement that brought him closer—until finally he stopped. Then she looked up at him, her face relaying a message that was a mixture of female pride and passionate longing. His eyes blazed with emerald fire and the pure intensity of male sexual arousal, burning the air between them.

Sam raised herself up on the tips of her toes, her lips parting on a shaky breath of urgent need, clinging to his robe as she did so to support herself. What she was inhaling and tasting now was an aphrodisiac far stronger than any wine.

He brushed her lips with his own, their touch warm and hard and yet exquisitely sensual and caressing, and then drew back to look at her. She moved closer, pressing herself to him in a silent plea for more. Lifting her face towards him, he kissed her briefly again, and then again, until finally he did what she knew she'd wanted him to do from the first and drew her to him in a kiss that possessed her as totally as the desert possessed those whose hearts it stole.

A commotion further down the corridor out of sight from them had them springing apart. Her face on fire, Sam fled, all too conscious of the fact that she was now going to be even later for her appointment than she had already been. Her heart was thumping with a mixture of shock and disbelief.

She was here in the Arabian Gulf on business, not to

behave in the reckless and out-of-character way in which she had just behaved.

Her impromptu trip out into the desert this morning might have increased her longing to get this job she had come so far to be interviewed for, but it had also meant that she had not really left herself enough time in which to get ready for the interview—which was why she had been hurrying at speed down the hotel corridor in the first place.

Now she had less than half an hour in which to shower and change and get to her appointment—and *that* was why her heart was thudding so fast and so erratically, not because of what had just happened with the man she had bumped into.

What on earth had come over her?

After all, she knew perfectly well that if anything it was even more pertinent in this part of the world than it was in the west for a woman who wanted to be taken seriously professionally and respected to behave in a way that did not compromise her status—with no inappropriate sexual behaviour towards Arab men.

And as, according to the lectures she had attended to prepare herself for this interview, inappropriate behaviour here in the Arabian Gulf could mean something as simple as a woman reaching out to touch a man on the arm, or engaging him in eye contact, what she had just done definitely came under the heading of *very* inappropriate behaviour indeed.

Even now, despite that knowledge, and despite the fact that normally she wouldn't have dreamed of acting as she had—would indeed have been shocked if anyone had suggested she might—she was still so aware of the swollen ache deep inside her that even breathing as hard as she was doing right now was enough to make her grit her teeth. Uncharacteristic longings seemed to have taken control of her thought-processes. Longings which were making her wish…

Wish what? That he had taken her to a bedroom and made mad, passionate love to her? A bedroom? Mad, passionate love? Who was she kidding? The kind of behaviour she had just indulged in was not conducive to that kind of encounter—and it would be naïve of her not to understand that. She was weaving ridiculous fantasies inside her head of mutual overwhelming passion at first sight.

She needed bringing her to her senses and some icy water throwing on the sexual heat that was now tormenting her.

What *was* this? She had heard that the desert could turn people crazy, but surely not after a mere couple of hours' viewing from the inside of a luxurious four-by-four air-conditioned vehicle? Oh, but he had been so handsome, and she had wanted him so much—still wanted him so much. She had never experienced anything remotely like the longing that had rolled over her when their bodies had made contact. It had been as though an electric surge of emotion had somehow bonded her to him, fusing them together, so that now she actually felt a physical pain, as though they had been forcibly wrenched apart.

One look into his eyes had been all it needed to complete her subjugation to what she had felt. If he had spoken to her then, and asked her to commit herself to him for the rest of her life, Sam suspected that she would quite willingly have agreed.

She tried to laugh herself out of her own emotional intensity, deriding herself for being silly and telling herself that she was probably simply suffering from too much sun. It wasn't much of an explanation for what she had felt, but it was way better than the alternative—which was to admit that with one single look she had fallen in love with a stranger to whom she would now be emotionally bound for ever.

CHAPTER ONE

VERE looked through the window of his office in the palace of Dhurahn, thinking not of the beauty of the gardens that lay within his view, which had been designed by his late mother, but of the desert that lay beyond them. The familiar fierce need that was stamped into his bones was currently possessing him. He wanted to put aside the cares and complexities of rulership of a modern Arab state and enjoy instead that part of his heritage that belonged to the desert and the men who loved it.

Which in one sense he would soon be doing. In one sense, maybe, but not wholly and freely. On this occasion it was his responsibility to his country and his people that was taking him into what was known as the 'empty quarter' of the desert, to the boundary they shared there with the two of their Gulf neighbours.

As he crossed to the other side of his office to look down into the courtyard, where his household were preparing for his departure, the remote and aloof air that was so much a part of him, which those who did not know him thought of as regal arrogance, was very much in evidence. Vere felt the weight of his responsibility towards the birthright he shared with his twin brother very deeply. He was, after all, the elder of the two of them, and his nature had always inclined him to take things more to heart and more seriously than Drax, his twin.

To Vere, ruling Dhurahn as their father and mother would have wished was a duty that was almost sacred.

There had only been one previous occasion on which his longing for the desert and the solace it offered him had been as strong as it was now, and that had been the time following the tragic death of his parents—his mother's passing having hit him particularly hard. That thought alone was enough to fill him with a savage determination to tighten his control over his current feelings, which he saw as a wholly unacceptable personal weakness.

It was unthinkable that his physical desire for the carnal pleasure afforded by one of those western women who came to the Gulf ready to trade their bodies for the lifestyle they thought their flesh could buy—a woman ready to give herself on the smallest pretext, shamelessly openly—should have driven him to the point where he felt his only escape from it could come from the same place where he had sought solace for the loss of his mother. It was more than unthinkable. It was a desecration, and a personal failure of the highest order.

It was more than half his own lifetime ago now since the death of their parents, but for Vere as a teenager, struggling to be a man and ultimately a ruler, with all the responsibilites that meant, the loss of the gentle Irish mother who had supplied the softening wisdom of her love against his desire to emulate his father's strength, had been one that had taken from him something very precious, leaving in its place a need to protect himself from ever having to endure such pain again.

Some men might think that for a man in his position the answer to the sexual hunger that was threatening to destroy his self-control was to satisfy it via marriage or a mistress.

His brother Drax was, after all, already married, with his wife expecting their first child in the near future, and Drax had hinted to him that he would like to see Vere married himself.

Vere frowned as he watched the four-by-fours being loaded for the long overland drive to the empty quarter.

The initiative prompted originally by the Ruler of Zuran, to investigate and if necessary redefine the old borders that separated their countries from one another, and from the empty quarter, was one he fully supported. They all in their different ways held certain territorial rights over the empty quarter, but by long-held and unwritten tradition they tended to ignore them in favour of the last of the traditional nomad tribes, who had for centuries called the empty quarter home.

The Ruler of Zuran wanted to bring the small band of nomadic tribespeople within the protection of the opportunities for education and health welfare he provided for his own people, and to this end he had contacted his neighbours: the Emir of Khulua, and Vere and Drax.

His initiative was one that was very close to Vere's own heart, provided it could be accomplished without depriving the tribes of their right to their own way of life. The Emir, not wanting to be excluded even though he was a more old-fashioned and traditional ruler, had also indicated that he wanted to be involved in the project, and as a first step the Ruler of Zuran had funded the cost of a team of cartographers to thoroughly map out the whole of the area.

It had been the Emir who had suggested that whilst this was being done it might be a good idea to reassess and establish their own individual borders with one another, which met at the empty quarter.

It was a good idea that made sense—as long as the Emir, who was known for his skill at adapting situations to suit his own ends, did not make use of the re-mapping to claim territory that was not strictly his. During private talks with the Ruler of Zuran, both he and Drax had agreed to keep a very strict eye on any attempts the Emir might make to do that. As part of their agreed preventative measures against this it had been decided that each ruler should take it in turn to be involved 'on the ground' with the project, and now it was Vere's turn to drive out to the border region of the empty quarter.

A movement on the balcony above him caused Vere to look upwards, to where his twin brother Drax and his wife Sadie were standing. The sight of their happiness and their love for one another touched a place inside him he hadn't known existed until Drax had fallen in love.

As twins they had naturally always been close, but the car accident that had killed their parents when the brothers were in their teens had made the bond between them even stronger. In the eyes of the world he, as the elder twin, was the one to step into their father's shoes, but both he and Drax knew that it had always been their father's intention that they would share the rulership and the responsibility for Dhurahn. However, every country was expected to have a single figurehead—and that duty rested with him.

Up until recently the duty had never been one he considered irksome. Where Drax embraced modernity, especially in architecture and design, he preferred to cling to tradition. Where Drax was an extrovert, he was more of an introvert. Where Drax enjoyed the buzz of busy civilisation, he preferred the silent solitude of the desert. They were as all those who knew them best often said, two halves of one whole.

Like many cultured Arab men, Vere revered poetry and studied the verse of the great poets, but just recently—although he hated having to admit it—the beauty of those words had brought him more pain than pleasure.

Normally he would have welcomed the chance to spend time in the desert, embracing the opportunity it gave him to be at one with his heritage, but now the knowledge of how close the desert was brought him to those things within himself that he felt the most need to guard. It was making him feel irritable and on edge.

Because he knew that being in the desert would exacerbate that sense of emptiness and loss that lay within him, and with it his vulnerability?

Vere swung round angrily, as though to turn his back on his own unwanted thoughts. His pride hated having to acknowledge any kind of flaw, and to Vere what he was experiencing was a weakness. He wanted to wrench it out of himself and then seal it away somewhere, deprived of anything to feed on so it would wither and die.

But, no matter how hard he fought to deny it any kind of legitimacy, every time he thought he had succeeded in destroying it, it returned—like a multi-headed monster, infuriating him with the mirror it kept holding up to him, reflecting back his faults.

Generations of proudly arrogant male blood ran through Vere's veins. The moral code of that blood was burned into him by his own will. He came from a race that knew the value of self-control, of abstinence, of starving the body and the spirit in the eternal battle to survive in a harsh desert environment. Real men, the kind of man Vere had always considered himself to be, did not allow uncontrolled hungers of any kind to rule them. Not ever.

And certainly not in a hotel corridor, with an unknown woman, and in such a way that—

He wheeled round again, his body tight with anger, ignoring the harsh glare of the sun as it fell across his face, highlighting the jut of his cheekbones and the searing intensity of his gaze. Not for Vere the protection of designer sunglasses to shadow and colour reality.

Lust must surely be the most despicable of all human vices. It was certainly the cause of a great deal of human misery. Vere had always considered himself above that kind of selfish weakness. As the Ruler of Dhurahn he had to be. And yet he could not escape from the knowledge that for handful of minutes he had been rendered so oblivious to his position by his own senses that nothing had mattered more to him than his desire for the woman he had held in his arms.

Another man might have shrugged his shoulders and accepted that he was a man, and thus vulnerable to the temptations of the flesh, but Vere's pride refused to accept that he was could be so vulnerable, so prone to human frailty. He had fallen below the demands he made upon himself to meet certain standards. Others might not condemn him for doing so, but Vere condemned himself.

He wasn't entirely alone, though, in his belief that a man needed to prove he could withstand the most rigorous of tests before he could call himself a man and a leader of other men. There was an 'other' to share his belief, and that 'other' was the desert.

The desert had a way of drawing out a man and highlighting both his strengths and his weaknesses. Normally Vere looked forward to the time he could spend in the desert as a means of replenishing his sense of what he truly was—but right now he wasn't sure that he wanted to submit his current state to that test. He had found himself wanting, and he feared that so too would the desert—that he would no longer be at one with it, just as he could no longer feel at one with himself.

More than anything he wanted and needed to dismiss the woman and the incident from his mind for ever—and then to deal with the damage she and it had done to his pride.

But the truth was he couldn't. The memory of her was branded into him and he couldn't seem to free himself from it—no matter how much he loathed and resented its presence. And her. He hadn't slept through a full night since it had happened. He didn't dare to let himself dream too deeply, fearing that if he did his dreams would be filled by her, and the ache of need he managed to control during the day would overpower him when he was asleep. It was bad enough having to acknowledge that every time he let his concentration slip the memory of her was there, waiting to taunt him. At its worst, that memory had him mentally lifting his hands to her body, determined to push her from him as he should have done all along, but knowing that in reality he would end up binding her to him.

How was it possible for one woman, a complete stranger, to invade the most private and strongly guarded recesses of his heart and mind and possess them, haunting and tormenting him almost beyond his own endurance?

It was mid-afternoon. He planned to leave for the desert camp of the surveyors as the sun began to set, so that he and his small entourage could make the most of the cooler night hours in which to travel. He had some work to do first, though, he reminded himself.

Whilst Drax and his wife occupied the new wing of the palace that Drax had designed for his own occupation before his marriage, Vere's personal apartments were in the older part of the palace, and had traditionally housed Dhurahn's rulers through several generations.

Thus it was that when he stood in the elegantly furnished and decorated private salon that lay behind the formal reception room where he held his public *divans*, to which his people were entitled to come and speak to him and be heard, he might be alone in the flesh, but in spirit the room was peopled with all those of his blood who had gone before him.

His formidable great-grandfather, who had ridden with Lawrence of Arabia and fought off all comers to maintain his right to his lands. His French grandmother, so elegant and cultured, who had bequeathed to him a love of art and design. And his own parents: his father, so very much everything that a true ruler should be—strong, wise, tender to those in his care—and his lovely laughing mother, who had filled his life with happiness and joy and the traditions of her homeland. Here in this room, at the heart of the palace and his life, he had always believed that he would never really be alone.

And yet now, thanks to one incident that was impossible to forget, that sense of comfort had been stolen from him and replaced with a stark awareness of his own inner solitude that he could not escape.

If he were reckless enough to close his eyes he knew that immediately he would be able to conjure up the feel of the thick silk of her wild curls beneath his hand, the scent of her woman's flesh—sweet and warm, like honey and almonds—the stifled heat of her breath when her body discovered the maleness of his own. And most of all her eyes, so darkly blue that they'd caught exactly the colour of the desert sky overhead just before the sun finally burned into the horizon. A man could lose his reason if he looked too long at such a sky, or into such eyes...

Was that what he believed had happened to him? Vere grimaced, bringing himself abruptly back to reality. He was a modern man, born in an age of facts and science. The fact that he had turned a corner in a hotel corridor and bumped into a young woman with whom he had shared a kiss—no matter how intensely passionate and intimate, no matter how bitterly regretted—hardly constituted an act of fate that had the power to change his whole life. Unless he himself allowed that to happen, Vere warned himself.

He strode across the room and pulled at the double doors that opened into the wide corridor beyond it, its floor tiled in the mosaic style that was true Arab fashion.

His parents had instituted a tradition that these rooms were the preserve of themselves and their children and no one else. Normally Vere relished that privacy, but now for some reason it irked him.

Was that the reason for the deep-rooted and ever-present

ache that pursued him even in his sleep? Tormenting him with images and memories—the smell of her, the feel of her in his arms, the feel of her body against his, the sound of her breathing, the scalding, almost unbearable heat of the moment their lips had met?

It was just a kiss—that was all… A mere kiss. A nothing—just like the woman with whom he had shared it. She hadn't even had the type of looks he found physically attractive. The type of women he liked to take to his bed were tall and soignée cool, worldly blondes—women who could satisfy him physically without involving him in the danger of them touching him emotionally.

Vere had never forgotten that loving a woman with the whole of his heart meant that ultimately he would be broken on the wheel of that love when she abandoned him. He had learned that with his mother's death, just as he had learned the pain that went with it. Better not to love at all ever again than to risk such agony a second time.

He still burned with shame to remember the nights he had woken from his sleep to find his face wet with tears and his mother's name on his lips. A man of fourteen did not cry like a child of four. Emotional weakness was something he had to burn out of himself, he had told himself. And that was exactly what he had done. Until a chance encounter in a hotel corridor had ripped off the mask he had gone through so much trouble to fix to himself, and revealed the unwanted need that was still inside him.

CHAPTER TWO

SAM stepped under the surprisingly sophisticated shower in the 'bathroom' compartment of the traditional black tent that was her current personal accommodation, soaping her body and taking care not to waste any water when she rinsed herself off—even though she had been assured that, thanks to the efficiency of the Ruler of Zuran's desalination plants in Zuran, there was no need for them to economise on the water that was driven in to the camp almost daily in huge containers.

Sam had been over the moon with joy when she'd learned that against all the odds she had secured this so coveted job of working as part of the team of cartographers, anthropologists, statisticians, geologists and historians brought together to embark on what must surely be one of the ambitious and altruistic ventures of its kind.

As a cartographer, Sam was part of the group that were remapping the borders and traditional camel caravan routes of this magical and ancient part of the world. Just the words 'the empty quarter' still brought a shiver of excitement down her spine. After all, hadn't her youthful desire to come to the Gulf initially sprung from reading about the likes of Gertrude Bell?

Normally Sam shared her comfortable and well-equipped accommodation with Talia Dean, one of the other three women who were also on the team, but the young American geologist had cut her foot two days ago, and was now hospitalised in Zuran.

Others before them had mapped the empty quarter and explored it, searching for hidden cities and routes, and the borders between the three Arabian states involved in the present exercise were already agreed and defined. However, modern technology combined with the excellent relations that existed between the three states meant that it was now possible, with satellite information combined with on-the-ground checks, to see what effect five decades of sandstorms that had passed since they were agreed might have had on the borders.

Now, with their evening meal over and the camp settling down for the night, Sam dried her newly showered body and then made her way into her blissfully air-conditioned tented bedroom.

Furnished with rich silk rugs and low beds piled high with velvet-covered cushions and throws, and scented with the most heavenly perfumes from swinging lanterns heated with charcoal, its combination of modern comfort-producing technology and traditional Bedouin tent produced an exotic if somewhat surreal luxury, which immediately struck the senses with its sharpness of contrast to the harshness of the desert itself.

But the desert also had its beauty. Some members of the team found the desert too harsh and unforgiving, but Sam loved it—even whilst she was awed by it. It possessed an arrogance that had already enslaved her, a ferocity that said *take me as I am, for I will not change.* There was something about it that was so eternal and powerful, so hauntingly beautiful, that just to look out on it brought a lump to her throat.

And yet the desert was also very cruel. She had seen falcons wheeling in the sky above the carcases of small animals, destroyed by the merciless heat of the sun. She had heard tales from the scarily expert Arab drivers supplied to the team, who were not allowed to drive themselves, of whole convoys being buried by sandstorms, never to be seen again, of oases there one day and gone the next, of tribes and the men who ruled them, so in tune with the savagery of the landscape in which they lived that they obeyed no law other than that of the desert itself.

One such leader was due to arrive in the camp tomorrow, according to the gossip she could not help but listen to. Prince Vereham al a' Karim bin Hakar, Ruler of Dhurahn, was by all accounts a man who was much admired and respected by other men. And desert men respected only those who had proved they were strong enough for the desert. Such men were a race apart, a chosen few, men who stood tall and proud.

She had been tired when she came to bed, but now—thanks to her own foolishness—she was wide awake, her body tormented by a familiar sweet, slow ache that was flowing through her as surely as the Dhurani River flowed from the High Plateau Mountains beyond the empty quarter, travelling many, many hundreds of miles before emerging in its Plutonian darkness into the State of Dhurahn.

Why didn't she think about and focus on *that*, instead

of on the memory of a kiss that by rights she should have forgotten weeks ago?

It had, after all, been three months—well, three months, one week and four and a half days, to be exact—since she had accidentally bumped into a robed stranger and ended up...

And ended up what? Obsessing about him three months later? How rational was that? It wasn't rational at all, was it? So they had shared an opportunistic kiss? No doubt both of them had been equally curious about and aroused by the cultural differences between them. At least that was what Sam was valiantly trying to tell herself. And perhaps she might have succeeded if she hadn't been idiotic enough immediately after the incident to fall into the hormone-baited trap of convincing herself that she had met and fallen in love with the one true love of her life, and that she was doomed to ache and yearn for him for the rest of her life.

What foolishness. A work of fiction worthy of any *Arabian Nights' Tale,* and even less realistic.

What had happened was an incident that at best should have simply been forgotten, and at worst should have caused her to feel a certain amount of shame.

Shame? For sharing a mere kiss with a stranger? That kind of thinking was totally archaic. Better and far more honest, surely, to admit the truth.

So what *was* the truth? That she had enjoyed the experience?

Enjoyed it?

If only it had been the kind of ephemeral, easy, lighter than light experience that could be dismissed as merely enjoyable.

But all it had been was a simple kiss, she told herself angrily.

A simple kiss was easily forgotten; it did not bury itself so deeply in the senses that just the act of breathing in an unguarded moment was enough to reawaken the feelings it had aroused. It did not wake a person from their sleep because she was drowning in the longing it had set free, like a subterranean river in full flood. It did not possess a person and her senses to the extent that she was possessed.

Here she went again, Sam recognised miserably. She was twenty-four years old—a qualified professional in a demanding profession, a woman who had so longed to train in her chosen field that she had deliberately refused to allow herself the distraction of emotional and physical relationships with the opposite sex, and had managed to do so without more than a few brief pangs of regret.

But now it was as though all she had denied herself had suddenly decided to fight back and demand recompense. As though the woman in her was demanding recompense for what she had been denied. Yes, that was it. That was the reason she was feeling the way she was, she decided with relief. What she was feeling had nothing really to do with the man himself, even though...

Even though what? Even though her body remembered every hard, lean line of his, every place it had touched his, every muscle, every breath, every pulse of the blood in his veins and the beat of his heart? And that was before she even began to think about his kiss, or the way she had felt as if fate had taken her by the hand and brought her face to face with her destiny and her soul mate. She was sure she would never have allowed herself to be subjected to such emotional intensity if she had stayed at home in England. Her loving but pragmatic parents, with their busy and practical lives, had certainly not brought her up to think in such terms.

If she was to re-experience that kiss now—that moment when she had looked into those green eyes and known that this was *it*, that neither she nor her life would ever be the same again, that somehow by some means beyond either her comprehension or her control, she was now *his*—it would probably not be anything like as erotic or all-powerful as she remembered. Imagination was a wonderful thing, she told herself. That she was still thinking about something she ought to have forgotten within hours of it happening only proved that she had far too much of that dangerous quality. After all, it wasn't as though she was ever likely to see him again—a stranger met by chance in a hotel corridor in a foreign country.

Instead of thinking about him, what she ought to be thinking about was tomorrow, when Sheikh Fasial bin Sadir, the cousin and representative of the Ruler of Zuran, who had been here at the camp since they had first arrived to oversee everything, would be handing over control of the project to Vereham al a' Karim bin Hakar, Sheikh of Dhurahn. In turn, in three months' time, he would be replaced by the nominated representative of the Emir of Khulua.

Sheikh Sadir was a career diplomat who had made it his business to ensure that both the camp and the work they were doing were run in a well-ordered and harmonious fashion. He had stressed to them—in perfect English—in an on-site briefing, that all three Rulers were determined to ensure that none of the small bands of nomads remaining in the empty quarter should in any way feel threatened by the work they were doing. That was why each working party would have with them an Arab guide, who would be able to speak with the nomads and reassure them about what was going on.

He had also gone on to tell them that whilst each state technically had rights over their own share of the empty quarter, where it came within their borders, it was accepted by all of them that the nomads had the right to roam freely across those borders.

Sam knew nothing about the Ruler of Dhurahn, but she certainly hoped he would prove to be as easy to work under as Sheikh Sadir. After all, she was already experiencing the problems that came with working alongside someone who was antagonistic towards her.

She gave a faint sigh. From the moment he had arrived four weeks ago, to take the place of one of the original members of the team who'd had to return home for personal reasons, James Reynolds had set out to wrong-foot her. He was two years her junior and newly qualified, and she had initially put his determination to question everything she said and did as a mere youthful desire to make his mark. So she hadn't checked him—more for the sake of his pride than anything else. She had assumed that he would soon realise that here they worked as a team, not as individuals trying to score points off one another, but instead of recognising that he was at fault James had started to become even more vocal in his criticism of her.

Sam really regretted ever having mentioned to James in conversation how interested she was in the origins of the river that flowed into and through Dhurahn. Since she had James had continually made references to it that implied she was spending the time she was paid for checking the status of the borders in trying, as James put it, 'to mess around with the source of a river that we all know is there', and in doing so avoiding doing any 'proper work'. Nothing could have been further from the truth.

'Take no notice of him,' Talia had tried to comfort her before she had injured herself. 'He obviously has issues with you, and that's his problem, not yours.'

'The trouble is that he's *making* it my problem,' Sam had told her. 'I really resent the way he's making such an issue of my interest in the source of the river—as though he thinks I've got some kind of ulterior motive.'

'I should just ignore him, if I were you,' Talia had told her. 'I mean, we've all heard the legend of how the river was first supposed to have been found—and who, in all honesty, wouldn't find it fascinating?'

Sam had nodded her head.

The story was that, centuries earlier, the forebears of Dhurahn's current Ruler, desert nomads, had been caught in a sandstorm and lost their way. After days of wandering in the desert, unable to find water, they had prayed to Allah to save them. When they had finished praying their leader had looked up and seen a bird perched on a rocky outcrop.

'Look,' he had commanded his people. 'Where there is life there must be water. Allah be praised!'

As he had spoken he had brought his fist down on a rock, and miraculously water had spouted from that rock to become a river that watered the whole of Dhurahn—the land he had claimed for his people.

'It's been proved now, of course, that the river runs underground for hundreds of miles before it reaches Dhurahn,' she'd reminded the other girl. 'The legend probably springs from the fact that a fissure of some kind must have allowed a spring to bubble up from underground. And luckily for Dhurahn it happened on their land.'

Dawn! Here in the desert it burst upon the senses fully formed, taking you hostage to its miracle, Vere acknowledged, as he brought his four-by-four to a halt so that he could watch it.

Naturally his was the first vehicle in the convoy, since it would be unthinkable for him to travel in anyone's dust. He had, in fact, left the others several miles behind him when he'd turned off the road that led to an oasis where the border-mapping team had set up camp, to drive across the desert itself instead.

As teenagers, both he and Drax had earned their spurs in the testosterone-fuelled young Arab male 'sport' of testing their skill against the treachery of the desert's sand dunes. Like others before them, they had both overturned a handful of times before they had truly mastered the art of dune driving—something which no one could do with the same panache as a desert-dwelling Arab.

These days, with modern GPS navigation systems, the old danger of losing one's bearings and dying from dehydration before one could be found wasn't the danger it had once been, but the desert itself could never be tamed.

The Oasis of the Doves, where the team was encamped, was just inside Dhurahn's own border, at the furthest end of a spear of Dhurahni land which contained the source of the river that made so much of Dhurahn the lushly rich land that it was.

Their ancestors had fought hard and long to establish and hold on to their right to the source of the river, and many bitter wars had been fought between Dhurahn and its neighbours over such a valuable asset before the Rulers had sat down together and reached a legal and binding agreement on where their borders were to be.

Vere could remember his father telling him with a rueful smile that the family story was that their great-grandfather had in part legally secured the all-important strip of land containing the beginnings of the river that they had claimed by right of legend for so many generations because he had fallen passionately in love with the daughter of the English diplomat who had been sent to oversee the negotiations— and she with him. Lord Alfred Saunders had quite naturally used his diplomatic powers in favour of his own daughter once he had realised that she could not be dissuaded from staying with the wild young Arab with whom she had fallen in love.

It had been at Vere's insistence that the scientific and mapping teams had been housed in the traditional black tents of the Bedou, instead of something more westernised. It might be Drax who was the artist, but Vere's own eye was very demanding, and the thought of seeing anything other than the traditional Bedou tents clustered around an oasis affronted his aesthetic sense of what was due to the desert.

He restarted the four-by-four's engine and eased it easily and confidently down the steep ravine that lay ahead of him. His mother had always loved this oasis, and it was now protected by new laws that had been brought in to ensure that it remained as it was and would never, as some oases had, become an over-developed tourist attraction.

The oasis itself was a deep pool of calm water that reflected the colour of the sky. It was fringed with graceful plants, and the narrow path that skirted it was shaded by palm trees. Migrating birds stopped there to rest and drink, the Bedou nomads drove their herds here, and held their annual trading fairs here. Bedou marriage feasts took place here.

It was a place for the celebration of life, symbolised by the oasis itself—the preserver of life. But for once being here was not soothing Vere.

Instead he felt hauntingly aware of an emptiness inside himself, and the ache that emptiness was causing. How was it possible for him to feel like this when it wasn't what he wanted? He had grown so used to believing that he could control his own emotions that he couldn't accept that somehow his emotional defences had been breached. It shouldn't have been possible, and because of that Vere was determined to believe that it *wasn't* possible.

The pain he had felt on losing his parents had shocked and frightened him—something that he had never admitted to anyone, not even Drax, and something he had tried to bury deep within himself. He had reasoned at the time that it was because his father's death had made him Dhurahn's new ruler—a role that demanded for the sake of his people that he show them that he was their strength, that they could rely on him as they had relied on his father. How could he manifest that strength when alone in his room at night he wept for the loss of his mother? For the sake of Dhurahn and his people he'd forced himself to separate from his love for his mother and the pain of his loss. He had decided there must be a weakness within him that meant he must never, ever allow himself to become emotionally vulnerable through love, for the sake of his duty. He couldn't trust himself to put his duty above his own personal feelings should he fall in love and marry and then for any reason lose the woman he loved.

Those feelings and that decision still held as good for him now as they had done the day he had made them, sitting alone in his mother's private garden, sick with longing for her comfort. His father had worshipped and adored their mother, but Vere knew that, had he survived the accident, he would somehow have continued to be the Ruler of Dhurahn, not a grieving husband, because that was his absolute and predestined duty. The weakness within him, Vere had decided that day, was one he must guard against all his life. And as a young, passionately intense and serious-minded teenager it had seemed to him that the only way he could guarantee to do this would be to lock the gates of his heart against the risks that would come with falling in love. He could not trust himself to have the strength to put duty before love. That was his secret shame, and one he spoke of to no one.

Now, the discovery that, after so many years of believing he had conquered and driven out of himself the emotions and needs he feared, he was aching constantly for a woman he had met fleetingly and only once, was creating inside him an armed phalanx of warrior-like hostile emotions. Chief amongst these was the inner voice that told him that the woman had deliberately set out to arouse him, and that his lust for her was unacceptable and contemptible.

* * *

Sam had woken up over an hour ago, with the first hint of dawn, and had been unable to get back to sleep. It would have been easy to blame her inability to sleep on the unease that James was causing her. Easy, but untrue, she admitted, as she pulled on the traditional black robe worn by Muslim women, which she had found so very useful as a form of protection against the sun and the sand.

She stepped barefoot out of the tent into the still coolness of the early morning.

Traditionally, all the members of a nomad tribe would have been up and busy at first light, to make the most of the cooler hours of the day before the sun rose too high in the sky for them to bear its heat, but in these days of air-conditioning units there was no need for anyone to rise early, and Sam knew from experience that she would have the early-morning peace of the oasis to herself.

A narrow pathway meandered along the water's edge, the ground flattened out in certain areas where animals came to drink. As Sam walked along the path a cloud of doves rose from the palm trees and then settled back down. A bird, so swift and graceful that all she saw was the flash of its wings, dipped down to the water and then rose up again with a small fish in its beak.

Sam turned a curve in the path and then came to such an abrupt halt that she almost fell over her own feet as she stared in disbelief at the man standing facing her. Her heart soared as easily as the doves on a surge of dizzying delight.

'You,' she breathed, helpless with longing.

CHAPTER THREE

WHAT a strange thing the senses were in the way they could instantly recognise a person and then immediately cause one's body to react to that recognition, Sam thought giddily, as she stared across the space that divided them at the man who was looking back at her.

She had known he was tall, but she had not realised quite how tall. She had known how virile and broad-shouldered and how muscular his body was, but not how strong and corded those muscles would be with the morning sun delineating the power beneath the flesh.

She hesitated, engulfed by the intensity of her own emotional and sexual arousal, and torn between flight from it and submission to it. Nothing remotely like this had ever happened to her before—which, of course, was why she had tried to initially evade and then deny it. Now, though, she was face-to-face—quite literally—with a truth she could not escape, with a knowledge about herself and her emotions, and she had no idea how to cope with it.

How was it possible for her to feel the way she did? How was it possible for her to want him so completely and unreservedly that all she wanted to do was go to him and give herself into his keeping for ever?

It was crazy, reckless….dangerous. And if she had any sense she wouldn't be thinking such things. She looked at his mouth. Sense. What was that? Nothing that mattered. Not like the aching sweetness pouring through her.

'How did you find me?' She was filled with awe and delight, humbled and elated. Reality belonged to another universe, not this magical place she had suddenly stepped into, where a person's most secret dreams could come true.

Perhaps she *was* dreaming? Only in daylight now, instead of during the protective darkness of the night hours. If so, Sam knew that she did not want to wake up again—ever. Why had she wasted all those hours trying uselessly to convince herself that nothing life-transforming had really happened between them? Why had she not had more faith in what she felt? He obviously had, because here he was. He had found her. He had come for her. Joy flooded through her.

Vere felt as though he had been turned to stone. No, not stone—because stone could not have felt what he was feeling right now. Stone could not have been pierced by the sharp, immediate and intense male surge of over-powering need to take her, to let his body satisfy the ele-mental force that was filling his head with images of their bodies together: naked flesh to naked flesh, her head thrown back in ecstasy whilst he moulded her to him, shaping her with his hands, spreading open the softness of her eager thighs, possessing her as she was begging him to do, endlessly and erotically, as she cried out to him over and over again in her pleasure until it became his, until he knew even as fulfilment rushed through him that its satisfaction would never be enough, that like a drug once tasted he would need more, and then still more.

The young boy's fear translated into a grown man's savage anger against what gripped him. He had to get away from her.

Sam could hardly contain her emotions. They made her tremble like a gazelle scenting the hunter and knowing its fate. In another minute he would reach her and take her in his arms, and then… She started to walk towards him, her pace quickening with the intensity of her need to touch him and be touched by him. A wild thrill of excitement shot through her—only to turn to a sharp stab of shocked disbelief when, just as she had almost reached him, he abruptly turned his back on her and started to walk away.

Pain and confusion swirled through her, leaving her feeling unsteady and insecure, desperate to stop him from leaving her.

'*No!*'

The denial felt as though it had been torn from her heart, it hurt so much.

Another man had appeared from a side path and was coming between them, bowing low in front of him, to murmur respectfully, 'Highness.'

Highness?

Had she actually whispered her appalled dismay? Was that why he had turned to look at her, that brilliant emerald-green gaze homing in on her, transfixing her to the spot, unable to move, unable to do anything, until it had been removed from her and the two men were walking away from her back down the path.

Sam searched her too pale expression in the mirror. If she didn't go and join the others soon, not only would she miss breakfast, she'd almost certainly have someone coming to ask why she wasn't there and if she was all right.

All right? She gave a small shiver. She wasn't sure she would ever be that again.

Had she actually seen him by the oasis, or had she only thought she had? Had he been merely a mirage, conjured up by her own imagination? And if he had, what did that tell her about the state she was in?

'Sam—at last. I was just about to come and look for you in case you'd overslept.'

The anxiety combined with just a hint of reproach in the voice of Anne Smith, the female half of a pair of married statisticians who were part of the team, caused Sam to give her an apologetic look.

'Sorry—' she began, but to her relief, before she was obliged to come up with an explanation as to why she was so late, Anne continued.

'You've never missed breakfast before, and with Sheikh Sadir telling us that the Ruler of Dhurahn has arrived, and that we are all to be formally presented to him, I was getting really worried that you wouldn't make it.'

At least now Sam knew the likely cause of his sudden reappearance here at the oasis—as well as the reason he had been in Zuran in the first place. He must be part of the Ruler of Dhurahn's entourage.

She had been in a total state of shock after seeing him so unexpectedly and then having him refuse to acknowledge her and walk away from her. It seemed ridiculous now that she had actually thought that somehow or other he had known she was there and come in search of her. Patently it was quite impossible—as she had since told herself. But at the time her sense of despairing anguish, coming so quickly on the heels of her earlier euphoria, had meant that it had been several minutes after he'd disappeared before she'd felt able to move. Even when she had, her heart had been thudding so heavily and uncomfortably that she had felt both sick and light-headed by the time she had reached the privacy of her tent.

Now she wasn't even sure she could trust herself to have actually seen him—not simply created the whole incident in the way that people lost in the desert and thirsting desperately for water saw mirages of what they so longed for.

The fact that she might be late for breakfast had been the last thing on her mind as she had semi-collapsed into a chair, her body going frantic with its wild message of longing, whilst her head and her heart burned with the pain of despair and humiliation.

Initially she had been glad that the shock of seeing him had left her so weak and shaky. If not for that, she suspected that her body, in its feverish heat of desire that seemed to have turned into a life force outside her own control, would have had her making a complete fool of herself and running

after him—or, just as bad, running after a mirage. It was hard
to say which would have offered her more humiliation.

Sam had stayed there in the chair for a long time, trying
to understand what was happening to her—and, just as importantly, why. She wasn't the sort of person who became
taken over either by an emotional or a sexual need so
strong that it possessed her and threatened her self-control.
How could one kiss be responsible for such a dramatic
change in her personality? How could it have her indulging in ridiculous fantasies of love at first sight and soul
mates?

Now she felt drained and on edge, exhausted physically
and emotionally by what had happened, as weak as though
she had been struck down by a powerful virus. Perhaps she
had, she thought wildly. Perhaps someone somewhere had
found the chemical formula that was responsible for sexual
attraction and was trying it out on unsuspecting victims,
causing them to suffer hallucinations.

Now she *was* being ridiculous, she warned herself as
she followed Anne to the large tent that was used for
meetings and general information announcements.

Anne, quite naturally, went to join her husband, who
was seated with their colleagues, leaving Sam to find her
own seat. Her heart sank when she saw that the only available space was next to James.

He gave her a superior look as she sat down next to him,
and Sam realised too late that virtually everyone else in the
tent was dressed formally—or at least as formally as the
their desert situation would allow. The men were in long
chinos and shirts, the women in sleeved tee shirts—some
of them had even covered their heads.

They had been told at their original orientation meeting that although the Sheikh of Zuran did not expect them to abide by the Arab rules of dress whilst working in the desert, the other leaders might.

Had something been said to indicate that the Ruler of Dhurahn *did* expect them to dress more formally? Sam wondered in dismay, now acutely conscious of her own sleeveless tee shirt, and her very practical below the knee loose-fit multi-pocketed cargo pants. She had a fold-up wide brimmed canvas hat in one of the pockets, but no headscarf. It was too late now, though, to worry about her appearance. Two men were being ushered onto the slightly raised platform with its traditional Arab divans.

One of them was Sheikh Sadir, and the other…

Sam's heart literally missed a full beat, staggered through a half-beat and then missed another—rather as though she were a boxer who had been knocked off his feet.

It couldn't be, surely? But it *was*; the man accompanying Sheikh Sadir, and who he was treating with such obvious reverence, was none other than the man she had seen earlier—the man with whom she had exchanged that shockingly intimate kiss in the hotel corridor in Zuran. So he wasn't a mirage, then. She didn't know now whether to be glad or sorry about that.

Now, of course, she truly understood the importance of that reverent 'Highness' that had so shocked her earlier.

She felt James nudge her hard in her ribs, and realised that everyone was standing and lowering their heads. Somehow she managed to get to her own feet in time to hear Sheikh Sadir introducing the man as Prince Vereham al a' Karim bin Hakar, the Ruler of Dhurahn.

The Ruler of Dhurahn—Prince Vereham al a' Karim bin Hakar.

Not a mirage. Not a mere *man* at all, but a prince.

Sam recoiled in shock. This couldn't be happening. But of course it was.

Now she knew exactly why he had turned his back on her on the path this morning. Of course he didn't want to acknowledge her. He was the Ruler of an Arab state and she was a nobody—less than a nobody in his estimation, no doubt. What he had taken from her he had taken as carelessly as he might have plucked a fig from a tree, biting into it in his desire to enjoy its sweetness and then discarding it, his enjoyment of it over and forgotten.

The robed serving staff provided by the Ruler of Zuran were coming round in pairs, one carrying a tray of coffee cups, the other a tray of coffee and small sweet pastries.

Up above them on the dais, the Ruler of Dhurahn was also being served with coffee. Sam watched as the sleeve of the gold-embroidered black robe he was wearing over an immaculate crisp white full-length Arab shirt was swept back, to reveal a lean brown hand and a muscular forearm. Beads of sweat pierced her forehead and her upper lip. She felt sick and shaky. It was because she hadn't eaten any breakfast, she tried to reassure herself. But she knew deep down that wasn't the reason at all.

'We'll see a bit more action now that he's here,' James told her, helping himself to several of the small pastries with relish. 'Word has it that he's got his own reasons for being here, and that he's the kind to make sure he gets what he wants.'

Yes, he was very definitely that kind, Sam agreed

mentally. And if he had wanted her... Stop that, she warned herself. Whatever foolish fantasies she might have entertained before—and they *had* been foolish—there could be no question of her continuing to entertain them now that she knew who he was.

He was standing up to speak, addressing them in unaccented crisply clear English as he reaffirmed what the cartographers amongst the team had already been told: namely, that the purpose of the exercise in which they ere involved was not either to reassess or challenge the validity of already existing borders but to study the effect of the desert itself on those borders.

'Curious that he seems so keen to warn us that we aren't to question the existing borders, don't you think?' James asked Sam *sotto voce*, under cover of eating yet another pastry.

'Not really,' Sam denied. 'After all, we were told right from the start why we are here and all he's doing is reaffirming that.'

She didn't want to have to listen to James, and she certainly didn't want him obstructing her view of the Prince And yet what was the point in her pathetic and painful desire to watch and listen to him, like an obsessed teenager fantasising about some out-of-reach pop idol?

Sheikh Sadir was now announcing that they were all to be presented to the Ruler of Dhurahn. Obediently everyone was shuffling out of their chairs to form a long line, going up to the dais being introduced.

'Here—hold this for me a minute, will you?'

Before she could stop him James had thrust the sticky crumb-filled plate from which he had been eating his pastries towards her, before standing up and leaving her holding it.

Sam looked yearningly towards the rear exit to the tent. She was closer to it than she was to the dais. It would be easy enough for her to slip away and avoid the formal introduction. But of course it was impossible for her to do that. Apart from anything else it would be a grave breach of protocol, and indeed almost an insult to the Ruler.

She looked with distaste at the plate she was still clutching and then, feeling a bit guilty, bent down to slip it beneath the nearest chair before filing into the queue behind James.

It would be her turn next. So far Sam had managed successfully to avoid looking directly at the new Ruler, but that hadn't stopped her heart thumping as heavily as though someone were wielding it like a sledgehammer, and now her palms were clammy with nervous perspiration. She was uncomfortably conscious of her bare shoulders and her casual attire. Would he think she had chosen to dress like this deliberately, as some kind of statement, or even worse in an attempt to lay claim to some kind of privileged status?

James was bowing his head. Sam heard him laugh, and then to her horror he turned to her and announced cheerfully,' If you'll take my advice, Prince, you'll keep an eye on my fellow cartographer here. She's already been checking up on the source of your river. The next thing you know she'll probably be challenging your borders as well. Trust a woman to want to meddle, eh?'

Sam could feel herself shaking with a mixture of disbelief and furious outrage at James's wholly unprofessional and untruthful allegations. With a few supposedly casual words he had painted a picture of her for the man who was now in charge of their venture that could only mark her out as a troublemaker, determined to ignore the guidelines they had been given from the start—guidelines which the man now staring very hard and very coldly at her had only just repeated.

The words *That's not true* hovered on her tongue, only to be choked back. Any kind of protest or argument from her now would only make her position worse.

Ignoring James, she made a determinedly low obeisance to the Prince and said quietly, 'Highness, I am aware, of course, of the purpose of our being here, and I thank you and the other Rulers for granting us the opportunity to work here. It is a unique opportunity and a privilege to be permitted to learn something of the mystery of the desert.'

Without waiting to see what kind of reaction her words were receiving Sam backed away, waiting until her place in front of the Ruler of Dhurahn had been taken by someone else before straightening up ready to turn round. But before she did so she couldn't prevent her gaze from seeking his. She wanted to look at him as the woman she had been in the hotel corridor, and him to be the man who had looked back at her with such fierce, sensual hunger.

He was not that man now, though. Now he was an Arab prince. The Ruler of an Arab State—a man, his dismissive gaze was telling her, as far removed from her as it was possible for him to be. His cold refusal to engage visually with her, never mind acknowledge or recognise her, confirmed everything that Sam had already guessed. He didn't want to know. The look he had given her earlier on the path confirmed that he had recognised her as immediately as she had done him, but now he was letting her know that he was the Ruler of Dhurahn and she was a European woman he wanted to pretend he had never met.

It was an indication of just how foolish she was that she actually felt achingly saddened to discover he was the kind of prince who was ready to enjoy the sexual advantages of his power and position in private, but at the same time determined to deny that he had availed himself of them in public.

All these weeks while she had been dreaming her stupid dreams, suffering her tormented longings, no doubt he had exorcised any desire she might have aroused in him speedily and effectively with someone else. Or maybe with several some one elses. No doubt to a man like him one woman was much the same as another—a piece of flesh to be used and then discarded.

It was relief that was burning that ice-cold fury into him, Vere told himself. Relief because now he had good reason—had he needed it, which he didn't—to treat her with disdain and suspicion, to make sure that he did not give in to his unwanted physical desire for her. And it was only physical, he assured himself.

Everyone had left the tent now, and Sam looked round for James. She might not have been able to say anything in front of their visitor, but she certainly intended to tackle James about the comments he had made—and sooner rather than later.

Once she could see him she made her way determinedly towards him, ignoring his cheerful, 'So, what do you think of our new boss, then?'

'Why did you try to give the Prince the impression that I've been questioning the legality of his country's rights to the river, when we both know that I haven't done any such thing?' she demanded coolly.

'Oh, come on. It was just a bit of banter that's all.' He shrugged and shook his head. 'What is it with you women that makes you take everything so ruddy seriously and go all hormonal and emotional?'

His jibe about her being emotional found its mark, but she wasn't going to let let him see that.

You've got equality now, you know,' he continued tauntingly. 'And that means—'

'I know exactly what equality means, James.' Sam stopped him, firmly taking charge of the conversation and fully intending to repeat her earlier demand that he explain his reasons for his comments to Prince Vereham. But before she could do so he had turned away from her to hail one of the other men.

A call for fellow male support? Sam wondered wryly, and her own inbuilt awareness of the bigger picture urged her to refrain from forcing a confrontation that could only lead to ill feeling. She had, after all, made her point and let him know that she was both aware of what he had done and annoyed about it. Involving herself in a battle of words that might descend into childish verbal gender taunts wouldn't do anything to enhance the professionalism on which she prided herself.

The triumphant smirk James was giving her still irked

her, though. He plainly thought he had got away with something—and if she was honest so did she.

But she wasn't here to indulge in petty squabbles with a colleague who seemed to have unresolved issues with working alongside women on an equal footing—and she was certainly not here to moon around thinking about a man who had unequivocally proved that he neither wanted anything to do with her nor would have been worthy of her if he had been.

With her back ramrod-stiff with determination and pride, Sam made her way back to her tent.

Knowing that today was the day when control of the venture was handed from Zuran to Dhurahn, she had deliberately planned not to go out in the field but instead to work on her computer, so that she could compare the information she had gathered on the ground with that picked up by the GPS systems overlooking the area. Only then would she be in a position to start preparing a comparison between what the landscape showed now and what had been recorded over fifty years ago.

The three Rulers had thought of everything that might be needed in a practical sense to make the venture a success, providing everyone with power and internet access for their computers, so that within minutes of entering her tent Sam should have been accessing the GPS information she needed.

Instead, though, she was typing into an internet search engine the name of the Ruler of Dhurahn…

CHAPTER FOUR.

THE formalities were over, and Sheikh Sadir and his entourage had taken their formal leave of him and begun their return journey to Zuran.

His own people were busy familiarising themselves with the site, and Vere had beside him the very latest printouts of the reports on various initiatives being undertaken by those working on the joint venture.

By rights he should be studying those reports. One of them, after all, could have grave repercussions for him and for his country. Instead he had been studying a plan of the camp and a list of those living in it.

Vere frowned and stood up, walked over to the exit of his personal quarters and pulled back the opening, causing the guard standing outside to jump to attention.

His own tent was set apart from the others, shielded from view by palm trees and close to the oasis, as befitted his status, with the tents of his private entourage surrounding it.

Beyond them were the tents of the team working on the project, arranged in a neat pattern, with wide walkways between them and those tents that housed the communal areas set in the centre. By Vere's reckoning, from the plan he had been studying, the tent housing Ms Sam McLellan was several rows away from his own but, like his, backed onto the oasis.

The last thing he had been prepared for when he had arrived here had been that he would see her. He had recognised her instantly, of course, and he could still feel the shock of that recognition deep down within his own flesh. As always, when he was reminded against his will of his reaction to the kiss they had shared, Vere was filled with a furious need to deny that it had had any kind of long-lasting effect on him at all. It was unthinkable that he, who abhorred the modern relaxed attitude towards casual throwaway sex, should have been involved in such a situation in the first place, and it was his weakness in allowing that to happen on which he needed to focus—not the irrelevant fact that, try as he might, he could not force his body to give up its physical memory of her.

Even harder to admit was the emotional impact the event had had on him, unleashing all the inner insecurity that the loss of his mother had brought him. *No!* Vere could feel the angry denial exploding inside himself. He felt as though he had been plunged into a war within himself and against himself.

He had something far more important to think about than his unwanted desire for Sam McLellan.

Drax had telephoned to tell him that he had received information that suggested that the Emir of Khulua intended to try and win a bargaining tool for himself in future negotiations between their two countries, by paying a member of the team assessing the changes within the desert boundaries to suggest that Dhurahn had laid claim to lands to which in reality it had no legal rights.

Of course, as Drax had said and Vere knew, the Emir had no intention of going so far as to try to make a claim on such lands. He was a very astute man, after all, and he knew that it would be impossible for him to make such a claim stick. However, what he could do was use the laws of Arab protocol and interaction, to put pressure on Dhurahn to make favourable concessions in his favour, as public recompense for and acknowledgement of 'past dues owed', which would tie them up in protracted useless negotiations for years to come. It was the kind of subtle game of politics and power that men like the Emir loved.

Vere knew that the Ruler of Zuran would not think too kindly of either of them if he were to be drawn into such a quarrel—especially if it affected the ongoing development of Zuran as a tourist destination. The situation that might develop would be one that would demand a considerable amount of time and subtle negotiation. However, with Dhurahn's bid to host the Arab world's first independent financial sector and stock market now accepted, but still in its all-important first year and being monitored closely, Vere knew they could not afford either the time to become engaged in delicate convoluted negotiations with the Emir, nor the fall-out effect on their reputation if an outright argument were forced on them by him should they refuse to bargain.

It seemed perfectly obvious to Vere that the person in the Emir's pay had to be Samantha McLellan. She, after all, was a cartographer, and responsible for mapping any changes in the shared boundaries. She had also, according to her colleague, already been spreading rumours about the validity of those boundaries—even if she herself had denied it.

It was surely a logical step from knowing that to working out that the supposed accidental meeting between them in Zuran, when she had bumped into him, had been no accident at all and instead had been deliberately contrived.

No doubt she had hoped to tempt him into a sexual liaison with her that would have allowed her to cloud the issue of the borders even more with planned lies. Perhaps claiming that Vere had admitted to her that there were irregularities with them.

It wouldn't matter that it was untrue. The Emir would still be able to use it in his Machiavellian plan to cause discord and discredit. Honour and good faith were vitally important in the Middle East, and once lost they were impossible to recover.

Had she really thought that he would be so easily taken in? That he would be deceived on the strength of one passionately sensual kiss and the feel of her body against his, combined with a look that suggested she had found her world in him?

How many other men had she practised that look on? Pain shot through him, splintering into shards of unexpected agony which he forced himself to bear as punishment for having dropped his guard long enough to have registered her lying eyes.

He was, though, completely safe from any kind of vulnerability towards her, knowing what he did. It was totally impossible and completely beneath him for him to desire her now. Her duplicity was his salvation. His salvation? His pride reacted as though it had been spurred. He had no need to seek salvation from the likes of Sam McLellan, a woman whose morals and whose flesh were up for sale. Again anger burned fiercely inside him because she had dared to think he might be gullible enough to be taken in by her and her risible attempt to foster a sexual intimacy between them that she could use to manipulate him.

She must have been furious when her colleague had betrayed her with his comment about her views on the true legality of Dhurahn's borders. Vere had no doubt that she must have been acting on the Emir's orders, trying none too subtly to lay the foundations for some kind of spurious claim about their border based on some farcical trumped-up evidence.

However, much as he longed to confront her with what he knew, Vere realised he could not do so. The first thing she would do would be to tell the Emir, and he and Drax were both agreed that their best course of action at the moment was to gather together as much evidence of the Emir's plans as they could and then confront him privately, having first laid the whole thing before the Ruler of Zuran. That way they could avoid humiliating the Emir in public, whilst making it plain that they had seen through his machinations.

Vere had no doubt that in such circumstances the Emir would be forced to back down—if only so that he could save his own face.

Meanwhile Vere knew that his duty to his country meant that he must do all he could to find out exactly what Samantha McLellan was doing. Once he had, he would need to get her to admit that she was being paid by the Emir to corrupt the details of her research in order to throw doubt on Dhurahn's original borders.

And there was only one realistic way in which he could do that, Vere thought cynically.

A woman like her, who had been bribed by one man, could be bribed by another to betray him. So, much as the thought revolted him, he would have to let her think that he was not averse to being propositioned by her, Vere decidedly grimly. He would have to act as though he wanted her—as if he was completely taken in by her.

Sam pushed the hair off her face and rubbed her eyes sleepily, before giving a shame-faced look at the screen in front of her. Had anyone told her four months ago that she would be doing something like this—scanning the internet and trying to pry into the private life of a man who had already made it clear that he wanted nothing whatsoever to do with her, a man who was a world away from the kind of man with whom she could realistically expect to share her life—she would have been appalled and defensive, instantly rejecting the very idea. She would have said, and genuinely believed, that she was far too well grounded, far too modern and way too practical to waste time doing something so pointless. Anyone who spent hours on the internet, pathetically prying into the life of a stranger, was surely to be pitied and told to get a life of their own.

What was it she was hoping to find out? She already knew exactly how he felt about her—or rather how he didn't. Trawling the internet wasn't going to alter that, given that he had made it so plain that he wanted nothing to do with her, was it?

Wasn't this the kind of thing that could lead to unhealthy and obsessive behaviour?

What did it matter what information about him the internet might hold? She had no intimate role to play in his life, nor he in hers.

Everything she was telling herself was quite true, Sam acknowledged, but she still couldn't quite bring herself not to give in to the temptation of looking. That was the trouble, wasn't it? she admitted to herself guiltily. Where he was concerned temptation seemed to be something she was incapable of resisting.

She had found any number of sites describing the history of the State of Dhurahn, but none of them contained any personal information about its current ruler.

She had also visited a site that gave a lavish description of Dhurahn's plans to create an independent Middle Eastern business and financial centre of excellence on land set aside for that purpose, complete with visuals of the office blocks and buildings. She had found, too, eloquent descriptions of the traditions of the country, preserved now and incorporated into national celebrations. There was even a piece about the current project, showing the original borders agreed when all three States had first been created.

But about Prince Vereham al a' Karim bin Hakar there was nothing—not even a photograph. Merely a clipped line in one of the free online encyclopaedias giving his date of birth, the names of his parents and grandparents, and the fact that the Rulers of Dhurahn had a tradition of choosing European women for their wives.

Sam's heart gave a small flurry of over-excited thuds as she re-read this information. *European* wives... Now she was being a fool.

Angry with herself for her silliness, she closed down the site and then opened up a new search for Khulua. Anne had mentioned that the state and its ancient ruins were well worth a visit. She had some leave days due in another month, and taking a short break away from the camp might do her good and bring her to her senses, Sam decided determinedly, as she checked out and then booked flights and a hotel for Khulua for a month ahead.

That done, Sam went to bring up the satellite map of the area which she used to work on.

As always when she studied this map, she was drawn to the area around the source of Dhurahn's river. She highlighted and magnified the river's source, fascinated all over again by her conviction that at some stage and for some reason the course of the river, not far from its source, had been changed. There might have been any number of reasons for this—none of them having any bearing on the state's border with Khulua—but Sam's natural curiosity burned to know exactly what that reason had been. Logically there was no reason why the original course of the Dhurani river should have been changed, which made her certainty that it had all the more mystifying.

The fact that Sam was engrossed in what she was doing, and had her back to the entrance to the tent, gave Vere the opportunity to stand and watch her unobserved before he started towards her.

As he began to walk in her direction, he knew he had certainly not made any sound that would have alerted her to his presence—and yet, as though he had commanded her to do so, within a heartbeat of him entering the tent she suddenly tensed and then swung round, saying, as she had done that morning when she had seen him by the oasis, '*You!* I mean… Your Highness,' Sam corrected herself quickly, half stumbling over the words as her brain struggled to come to grips with the fact that she had known he was there without hearing him or seeing him.

Her heart was thudding into her ribs so heavily that it almost hurt, and it was certainly making her feel weak and light-headed—or maybe that was caused by the fact that suddenly there didn't seem to be enough air in the tent for her to breathe properly, and what air there was had turned warmer, somehow, pressing against her and bringing with it unwanted memories of their first meeting.

Sam prayed that he wouldn't come any closer. She was already acutely aware of the sound of his breathing and the scent of his body. In trying to avoid looking into his eyes she had instead focused straight ahead. Now, though, she recognised that this was a mistake—because her eyes had impacted on his hands, strong and sinewy, with long fingers, hands that could easily support the weight of a hunting falcon, or secure the trembling body of a yearning woman. She was starting to tremble, sweat beading her forehead as unwanted images crashed through her defences. She didn't think she could bear this. She really didn't. But she must—or else risk giving him the opportunity to snub her again the way he had done earlier.

'I wanted to talk with you about this claim made by your colleague that you are questioning the authenticity of

Dhurahn's borders,' Vere announced coldly, without preamble.

His heart was thudding like blows on an anvil delivered with a heavy hand. It was anger that was responsible for the way he was feeling. Nothing else. There could not be any other reason. Gifted as he was with the keen eyesight that belonged to men of the desert, from where he had been standing he had seen her booking a flight to Khulua, thus confirming everything he had suspected.

Sam, though, was oblivious to what was going through Vere's mind. All she could focus on was her own misery and the situation she was in. She had feared, of course, that as Dhurahn's Ruler he *would* challenge her about James's comment, but she had assumed that it would be in a more formal setting. She had thought that he would send for her, perhaps, and demand that she explain herself—rather than seek her out on his own, and in the privacy of her own quarters, where she was far too aware of him as a man to be able to concentrate on his status.

He was wearing that same fresh cologne he had been wearing before and it was distracting her, painting images into her thoughts that had no right to be there, and which were certainly not appropriate for their current meeting. She struggled to dismiss them and failed. She knew that if she let her concentration slip even for a second she would be remembering how it felt to be in his arms. And longing to be there again, despite what she knew? No, she denied immediately. But she knew she was lying to herself.

'I have never questioned Dhurahn's borders,' she told him truthfully.

'No? That was not the opinion of your colleague.'

She could see a glint of angry contempt in the gaze he was fixing on her. It drove her to defend herself.

'I have never questioned Dhurahn's borders, either publicly or privately.' she repeated, determinedly and fiercely.

His anger wasn't abating, and to her chagrin she heard herself continuing so weakly that she might just as well have been pleading with him for understanding.

'I don't think James realised how serious… That is to say, I think he was just making conversation…There is no valid reason why he should have said what he did.'

That wasn't the truth, was it? she challenged herself inwardly—and guiltily. Although it upset her to think it, she suspected that James had wanted to get her into trouble, and had said what he had deliberately, because of his own personal and unadmitted agenda.

She could see, though, that this man would never believe she was merely an innocent victim, and that he wasn't prepared to give her the benefit of the doubt. Not when she was pretty sure that he was already blaming her for another incident.

And did *she* think she was blameless there as well? Had she done everything she possibly could to avoid the intimacy they had shared? Had it all been down to him and him alone? Sam could feel her conscience prodding her. No, she didn't think that. Not after the way she had felt and behaved. But equally, if she wasn't blameless, then neither was all the blame hers either, was it? No matter how Prince Vereham al a' Karim bin Hakar was choosing to act now.

'James misunderstood what I was trying to say,' she

added, for further emphasis of her point—even though she already knew that he wasn't really interested in giving her the opportunity to defend herself.

She could see that he was looking past her towards her computer, his frown deepening. For a moment, to her horror, she thought she might inadvertently have brought up one of the searches she had been doing on him, but when she glanced at the screen she was relieved to see that all it contained was her map of the source of the river.

He strode past her to focus on the screen.

'This is the source of the Dhurahni river.'

It was a statement more than a question.

'Yes,' Sam agreed.

'Why are you studying it? It flows quite plainly through Dhurahn, and only Dhurahn, and is therefore outside your remit for exploration and examination.' His voice was clipped, his manner hostile.

'Yes, I know,' Sam was forced to admit.

'So explain to me what this is all about.'

He wasn't just hostile, he was furious as well, Sam recognised miserably. But her tormentor hadn't finished.

'Why exactly do you feel it necessary to question the Dhurani River's source?' he continued angrily. 'What are you hoping to prove, or gain. And why? What is the agenda behind this underhanded delving into something which has nothing whatsoever to do with you?'

Sam stared at him in horrified dismay.

'No—please, you don't understand,' she protested 'It isn't like that. It was just that…that I couldn't resist…' She could feel her face starting to burn as she realised the danger she was getting herself into. 'There's something about underground rivers that is so fascinating—especially those that travel so far—and I…'

Vere looked at her.

'It seems to me that you have a penchant for not resisting your own desires, Ms McLellan. Regardless of whether or not in doing so you are transgressing set boundaries.'

His words weren't just meant to refer to the river, Sam knew, and her face burned even more uncomfortably.

'There's no law that says that a person can't take an interest in natural phenomena,' she told him, somehow managing to find the gritty courage to reply in his own subtle double-speak. There—let him make what he wanted of that! 'Especially when I'm only doing it in my own time.'

Vere's mouth hardened, but he didn't say anything. It had been a mistake to let his emotions get the better of him. He had put her on her guard now, and it was unlikely that he was going to get her to admit that she was being paid to cause trouble for Dhurahn.

'I don't see why I shouldn't be interested in the river,' Sam continued determinedly. 'It's a vitally important resource for the area, after all, and I admit that I am curious about the fact that at some stage the course of the river appears to have been changed.'

'As you've just acknowledged, you are perfectly well aware that the river, and whatever may have happened to it, lies within Dhurahn's borders, and is therefore outside your mapping remit,' Vere told her coldly.

'Yes…' Sam was forced to admit.

'You are a professional cartographer. Don't think I would be the only person to question this excuse of "curiosity" you have given me.'

He was surely far more angry than the situation merited. He was so angry, in fact, that she could almost feel his fury raising the temperature inside the tent, and Sam had no illusions about the extent of the trouble she was in. He had spoken of her having an agenda, but Sam believed that any agenda belonged to *him* and related to what had happened between them. Was he looking for an excuse to have her dismissed? Removed from the camp and thus his vicinity?

'It is just curiosity. It is interesting, and—' she began to insist, only to have him cut her off with his savage voice.

'Interesting? To study and question something you have not been asked to involve yourself in—and I suspect using equipment and time that should have been used for something else? Interesting to whom, I wonder?'

He was losing it, Vere recognised. Going in a reckless headlong charge too far down a road that was strewn with potential hazards. But somehow he hadn't been able to stop himself. And he knew why. Despite the fact that he both wanted and needed to believe that this woman was someone he could not trust, against all the odds—against everything he had trained himself to think and be—something deep within him wanted to believe otherwise.

It was something he must root out and destroy.

Sam could feel the shock of his antagonism ricocheting through her. Despite the fact that he was wearing traditional Arab dress, any resemblance to some romantic image of a desert prince her imagination might once have conjured up collapsed like the fiction it was. Now that she was confronted with the reality, she could see a very twenty-first century, hard-edged and angry dominant male, ready to do battle for what he considered to be his. She suspected that if she didn't do something, and soon, she was going to find herself out of a job.

'I'm sorry if…if I've caused offence, or…or broken any rules.' She forced herself to apologise, inwardly hating having to be so submissive. But she didn't want to damage her career, and she wasn't going to let him penalise her just because he regretted what had happened in Zuran.

Did he think she didn't regret it even more? Did the sharp look he was giving her mean that he was aware that her apology might relate to more than her transgression over the possible diversion of the river?

'Where exactly is this supposed alteration of the course of the river? Show me,' Vere commanded, without making any response to her apology. He knew that he ought to be focusing on the plan he had made to win her over, instead of allowing his own revulsion at the thought that he might have revealed some vulnerability to her to drive his reactions.

He was standing far too close to her, Sam thought shakily, as she glanced at one of his hands on the back of her chair, and then at the palm of the other, flat on the small desk next to her computer.

She wasn't obliged to do as he was demanding. She could ask him to leave. He was, after all, in her private quarters, and she wasn't sure just how long her self-control could endure this sort of pressure.

As he himself had just pointed out, the information she had gathered was outside her working remit, and therefore she was under no obligation to share it with anyone. However, common sense told her that it would be extremely foolhardy of her to say as much. So, instead, she reached for her mouse and highlighted the area she had been examining, trying not to let her hand shake as she did so.

It was disconcerting having him stand half behind her and so close to her. More than disconcerting. She could feel the warmth of his breath against her skin as he leaned forward to take a closer look at the screen. It sent a frisson of unwanted sensual pleasure shivering over her skin, making her tense herself against its effect. She was aware, too, of the heat of his body and its maleness. And of the effect that maleness had already had on her. *Was* she aware of that, and the risk that came with it of humiliating herself a second time?

Sam was certainly conscious of the sharpness of the inner warning voice that was asking her that question, but at the same time another voice was whispering to her far more seductively that if she leaned back now her head would be resting against his shoulder, and then if he placed his hand on *her* shoulder he could turn her towards him…

Abruptly, something that was both a physical ache of longing and emotional anger against it jerked though her body and tightened. It was impossible for her to allow herself to feel and think like this. What had happened to her normal level headed common sense and dignity? It had been bad enough when she had been daydreaming about him, believing that he had shared her desire, but now she knew the truth her pride alone should be sufficient to stamp out any lingering feelings of physical longing she might have.

'It's here that I first noticed something,' she told him, somehow managing to sound far more in control and professional than she felt as she indicated the darker markings that showed where the channel was. But did her voice sound as thin with tension to him as it did to her? Had he noticed that her arm was stiff from the effort it took her to keep it out of contact with him whilst she moved the mouse?

Vere could have sworn that he was only looking at the screen, but somehow he could also see the soft fullness of her mouth, and the way her lips parted as she drew in that small shallow breath. Her breasts lifted. Soft, naturally curved breasts that made a man ache to cup his hands around them.

Furious with himself for the direction his thoughts were taking, Vere took refuge in attack.

'Do you seriously expect me to believe that a few scratches on a map are serious evidence of someone having tampered with the course of a river as fast-flowing as the Dhurani?' he derided.

'These are GPS images,' Sam reminded him, stung by his criticism. 'Naturally they aren't easy to read, especially to the untrained eye.'

She was rewarded with a swift annihilating glance.

'I assure you that I am more than familiar enough with satellite images to be able to translate what these mean,' he said coldly.

'Then you will understand that the extent of the channel is much more defined when seen on the ground,' Sam retorted firmly, determined to show him that she was not going to be bullied out of her professional opinion.

'I am familiar with the source of the river, and I cannot say that I have ever noticed.' Now his tone was coldly dismissive.

It was plain that he did not like what she was saying, Sam recognised.

'Then perhaps you weren't looking in the right place.'

Or maybe he hadn't wanted to notice? Sam thought inwardly, wondering at the same time why this might be. After all, as he had said, both channels lay within the boundaries of Dhurahn, and it could not be disputed that the river ran exclusively through Dhurahn's land. But in some ways that made the fact that she was sure it had been altered all the more fascinating—at least to her.

She could feel the faint draught as he released the back of her chair before striding past her, turning round abruptly to face her, and then saying sharply, 'Maybe not.'

He was, Sam noticed, looking at his watch. She started to exhale unevenly in relief, assuming that he was about to leave, but instead to her dismay he informed her, 'After the evening meal tonight we shall drive out to the source of the river. It is a three-hour drive, and we shall camp there overnight. In the morning you can show me this supposed channel, and then we can return before the heat of the day.'

'No…' Sam croaked, panic gripping her. Her reaction was an immediate and instinctive grab for self-protection. *'What?'*

It was plain from both his expression and the disbelief in his voice that he wasn't used to having his orders questioned, Sam recognised, and now he was coming towards her.

Her panic increased, but shamefully now it was joined by another emotion—and this one was telling her that what she really wanted was for him to come even closer.

'No,' she repeated, denying her own emotions as much as his demand, as unwanted need threatened to swamp her protective panic. 'Don't come any closer…don't…. don't touch me.'

Wasn't what she really meant, *do* touch me—oh, please, please *do* touch me, and keep on touching me for ever…?

He had come to an abrupt halt several feet away from her and was looking at her as though she were an insect that had crawled out from beneath a stone, Sam thought. As though she were something unclean.

'Don't touch you?' he repeated, as though he could hardly believe she had spoken those words to him. 'Do you dare to believe that I would wish to?'

Torn between angry pride and stinging humiliation, Sam longed to have the kind of thick skin that would have enabled her to point out to him that there had been an occasion when he had done rather a lot more than merely touch her. But her own feelings of shamed guilt about the part she had played in that incident held her back, so instead she stayed silent. She wished she had not done so when he continued coldly, 'Well let me assure you that you need have no fear on that account. And before you humiliate yourself by referring to a certain incident that does neither of us any credit, let me tell you that it is certainly something I intend to forget. I would advise you to do the same.'

'There's no need to advise me to do anything. I had already forgotten it, Your Highness,' Sam lied through gritted teeth in fierce retaliation.

Her vehemence caught Vere off guard. He wasn't used to being challenged in any way or by anyone—except oc-

casionally Drax. The fact that she had done so, and with
such furious passion, was an unfamiliar enough experience
for him without the additional unwanted knowledge that
it underlined the fact that this woman seemed to have the
knack of reacting in a way that he just wasn't prepared for.
Even worse, she provoked him into behaving in a way that
was totally out of character for him.

He had come in here with one purpose in mind, and that
had been to get her off her guard enough for him to find a
way to circumvent whatever it was the Emir was planning
to do. Instead she had somehow or other forced him into
a role that was a total surprise to him—and not a pleasant
one either.

Vere did not like those kind of surprises. He liked to feel
that he had the ability to read both situations and people
well enough to be one step ahead of them, and thus
prepared for what might happen. Sam's stubborn refusal
to fit into the mould he had cast for her was infuriating.

She was lying about having forgotten their first meeting,
of course. It was ridiculously obvious in everything she
said and did, in every look she gave him, that she remembered it very well. He had a good mind to make her admit
that to him—as well as admit why it had happened. Did
she think he was a complete fool? Vere raged inwardly, his
anger growing. Or did she think that by her pretence she
could whet his appetite for more of the same?

Had she been lying in wait for him on that corridor? Had
she believed that he would fall for that kind of ploy? Did
she really think he was so emotionally vulnerable that he
would be taken in by her and want her? Did she think that
he was the kind of man who was so lacking in principles

and pride that he would want what she had been so ready to offer?

Well, if so, she was certainly going to learn now how wrong she was and how totally immune he was to her, he decided furiously, and he strode past her and out of the tent. He ignored the inner voice trying to reason with him and remind him that he was supposed to be winning her confidence and getting under her guard.

CHAPTER FIVE

'SAM. There you are—could I have a word?'

Sam jumped guiltily. She had been so engrossed in her own thoughts—thoughts which revolved totally around having a certain person on his knees, begging her forgiveness for misjudging her—that she hadn't even heard Anne coming towards her until the other woman had spoken to her.

'Yes. Of course…'

'It's about James,' Anne confided, drawing her to one side as other members of the team walked past them on their way to the communal dining area for their evening meal.

'Ted thinks that he's been bringing alcohol into the camp and drinking it. He says he could smell it on James's breath the other morning, and he thinks he saw him drinking from a hip flask when they were out in the field, although of course he can't prove it.'

Sam could hear the dismay in Anne's voice.

'Oh, surely not,' she protested. 'We all know now that having alcohol here even for our own consumption is strictly forbidden. That was made plain to all of us when we were interviewed. James is very ambitious, and I can't see him doing anything that would damage his career.'

'Well, one would certainly like to think not—which is why Ted is so concerned about him. Ted and I have spent a lot of time working in the Middle East, and I'm afraid that we have seen colleagues before develop a drink problem whilst they're out here, away from home. He's worried that James could be heading in that direction.'

'Just because Ted saw him drinking alcohol that doesn't mean he has a drink problem,' Sam felt bound to point out—although just why she should be defending James after the trouble he had got her into she had no idea.

'Of course not. But as I said Ted says there have been a couple of occasions on which he's been pretty sure he could smell drink on James's breath. He has tried to talk to him about it, but James brushed him off. In fact he was quite rude. I don't know if you've noticed, but sometimes his behaviour seems to be quite irrational. Neither of us likes telling tales out of school, but since you're working with him we agreed that we should have a word with you.'

'I'm glad you have,' Sam admitted. 'Not that there's anything I can do if he is drinking. I'm the last person he'd be likely to listen to.'

'Well, yes, but to be honest it was you we were thinking about rather than him. He does rather have a down on you. It was remarkably tactless of him to make the comment he did to the the Prince.'

'Yes,' Sam agreed ruefully. 'It was—especially as it wasn't even true.'

What she wasn't going to say to Anne was that she was beginning to wonder if James had been going through her work behind her back and had come across the satellite images of the river. From now on she intended to be far more careful about the access he had to her papers and her computer. Little as she liked to think he was looking for a means of getting her into trouble, she suspected that was exactly what he *was* doing—although she had no real idea why. If he did indeed have a drink problem then she genuinely felt very sorry for him. But she also knew that it was professional help he needed, not her sympathy.

'Come on—we'd better go and get some dinner. Have you heard yet when Talia is likely to be back?' Anne asked.

Sam shook her head. 'It's going to be several weeks, but more than that I don't know.'

The Smiths were a kind and thoughtful couple, and she appreciated the fact that, knowing she was now without a female companion, Anne had asked her to join them to eat. Not that she felt hungry. Not when she knew that after their evening meal she was going to have to give in to the demands of Prince Vereham al a' Karim bin Hakar and show him what she had discovered.

'I must say that I've never been on any field trip where we've been fed so well.' Anne laughed. 'I think I've actually put on weight.'

'The food *is* excellent,' Sam agreed.

Zuran was a world-renowned luxury holiday destination, and the Ruler of Zuran had provided them with the services of a gifted young chef. Fresh food was brought out for them every day, along with water, and Sam could well understand why Anne felt she'd gained a few pounds.

'I treated myself to a copy of the new Jane Austen DVD whilst we were in Zuran, but it's not Ted's cup of tea—so if you'd like to watch it with me after dinner...?' she offered.

'I'd love to,' Sam said truthfully. 'But I'm afraid I can't.' Trying not to sound as self-conscious as she felt, she told Anne, ' Prince Vereham al a' Karim bin Hakar has ordered me to accompany him on a field trip, and he wants to set off after dinner.'

If Anne was surprised, to Sam's relief she managed to keep it to herself, saying easily, 'Well never mind. Perhaps another time.'

There was no sign of James in the large air-conditioned tented 'dining room', nor any sign of the Ruler of Dhurahn either—but then it wasn't unusual for the high-ranking Arabs monitoring their work to eat separately from them. And of course Sam was relieved and delighted that he wasn't there. The last thing she wanted was to look up from her food to find that merciless cold green gaze focused on her.

'Finished already?' Anne asked in surprise, when Sam touched her on the arm a little later, and explained that she was leaving.

'I've got to put a few things together. Somehow I don't think it would be a good idea to keep the Prince and his entourage waiting.'

'No,' Anne agreed. 'I don't think it would. I must say he is an outstandingly autocratically handsome man—very compelling, if somewhat austere, plus he has such presence. Jane Austen, I think, would have had a field-day with such a role model for a hero. You'd never think to look at him that Dhurahn is the most forward-thinking and democratically run Gulf State of them all, but Ted says that it is.'

Forward-thinking and democratic? No, she would certainly never have thought of describing the Ruler of Dhurahn as either of those things, Sam acknowledged grimly as she made her way back to her quarters to collect her laptop and everything else she felt she might need for her upcoming trip. Her *trip*? Didn't she mean her ordeal? Sam asked herself wryly.

Vere looked at his watch. His men should have loaded up the four-by-four with everything they would need by now. He had spoken to Drax and explained to his twin what he had discovered, and Drax had promised to find out what he could about Ms Samantha McLellan.

It was only after he had ended the call that Vere realised he had said nothing to Drax about his own original meeting with 'Sam', as her colleagues appeared to call her. But then why should he? What possible relevance to what was happening now could that have? None whatsoever—other than to underline for him the type of woman she was and keep him on his guard against her.

A fresh surge of outrage and pride-fuelled fury burst through him as he recalled how earlier in her tent she had tried to pretend that she thought he had been going to touch her. Did she really think she had the power to drive him into such a state of arousal and need that he would do such a thing. A man in his position? He could almost hear his twin's soft laughter at his indignation. A small rueful smile curled his mouth. Drax had always had the knack of softening the burden imposed on him by his position. But the reality was that he was not just a man, he was Dhurahn's ruler, and he had a duty to set his people the right kind of example. He couldn't, for example, imagine his father, who had been so strong and so noble, indulging in the kind of behaviour *he* had descended to. But then his father had had his mother, and the love they had shared had been plain for everyone to see.

Love. He must never fall in love. Imagine, for instance, if those hot, sharp pangs he had felt when he had held Ms Samantha McLellan in his arms had not been lust but love? How would he be feeling right now?

What? What was this? What on earth was he doing, coupling Samantha McLellan and the word love together in the same sentence?

'Everything is ready, Highness.'

Vere acknowledged the soft words of the man who had just salaamed his way into his tent with a brief nod of his head.

Sam had just finished packing a change of clothes into her backpack when the flap entrance to her tent was flung back to admit the Prince.

His curt, 'You are ready?' caused her to respond to him with an equally curt inclination of her head.

'Very well, then.'

He turned to leave, plainly expecting her to follow him, so Sam picked up her things and hurried after him. Irritatingly, the narrowness of the path and the bulk of what she was carrying made it impossible for her to do anything other than walk behind him, for all the world as though she was acknowledging his sexual superiority to her and following tamely. That was something she would certainly *never* do, she fumed, so engrossed in her own anger that she only just managed to stop herself from cannoning into him when he stopped alongside a large four-by-four. Bumping into him a second time was the last thing she needed to do right now—especially after his previous accusation.

Obviously he would be the one travelling in this enormous monster of a gas-guzzler, Sam decided, and searched round for the rest of the vehicles, looking confused when she couldn't see any.

'Something is wrong?' he was asking her impatiently.

Yes, just about everything, Sam thought ruefully, but shook her head and said instead, 'No.'

'Excellent. Give me your things, then, I'll put them in the back.'

Give *him* her things and *he* would put them in the back? Sam knew she was gaping at him as he took the laptop case from her unresisting grip. He was a prince, the Ruler of an Arab state. He was arrogant and demanding, and he was used to being waited on hand and foot, so no way could he have meant what he had said. But apparently he had, Sam realised, as he gestured to her to remove her backpack and then took it from her, carrying it as though it weighed nothing instead of the several heavy kilos her shoulders knew it did.

She could hear him opening the rear door of the four-by-four and then closing it again. He strode to the passenger door ignoring her. Sam looked wildly around herself wondering where on earth the vehicle that was to be her transport was, and if he would actually allow his own driver to drive off without her.

'If you're ready?'

It was more an impatient command than a request. Confused, Sam looked from his irritated stance beside the passenger door he was holding open to the empty seat, and then back to him again.

'You want me to get in?' she asked him

'It would seem a logical process, if we are to leave for our destination,' he agreed.

From the way he was looking at her, if she kept him waiting much longer he'd be bustling her into the passenger seat like a small child, Sam suspected, reluctantly stepping up to the door. Her, 'What about you?' was lost in the heavy thud of the door being closed by an impatient male hand.

She was reaching for her seat belt when the driver's door opened and he swung himself into the driver's seat, closing his own door as he did so.

He was driving them himself?

'What's wrong?'

'Where are the others?' she asked uncertainly.

'What others?'

'You mean that… But I thought…'

'You thought what? That after your earlier crass attempt to foster intimacy between us I wouldn't want to risk being alone with you? Somehow I think I'm capable of defending my own honour.'

Sam could feel her face burning with fury. She looked towards the door of the now moving vehicle, but of course it was too late for her to register a protest by trying to get out and walk off.

'What happened in that corridor was an accident…a mistake…'

'A mistake—yes, I agree. But an accident?'

'And as for you worrying about risking being alone with me—' She was so angry that the words she wanted to say had balled up as tightly in her throat as her fingers moved into tight fists against her palms. 'That is both offensive and ridiculous. After all, I'm not the one who arranged this trip, and I certainly wouldn't have chosen to make it alone with you.'

Vere knew perfectly well that she had a point, but the fact that she had made it still angered him. In fact, everything about her and her presence here, and the problems she was causing, infuriated him.

Her meddling in something that was nothing whatever to do with her, and her ridiculous claims about the source of the river, were obliging him to take time out of his already very busy life to check up on the situation, ready to head off any arguments the Emir might try to put forward.

He had no desire whatsoever to have her ideas brought into a more public arena, for others with their own agendas to get involved, and because of that he had been forced to make this trip alone with her—something he would never ordinarily have done.

When he came to the desert he liked to come alone—completely alone—so that he could replenish himself via his solitude with it.

He disliked sharing the desert—'his' desert—with anyone, but the thought of having to share it with this woman, who had already aggravated and irritated him to the point where he couldn't even close his eyes in sleep without her appearing in his dreams to infuriate him, inflamed his hostility towards her like a bur under a saddle. He came to the desert to cool his overheated thoughts and emotions, to live for a precious few days as a poet hermit, letting the desert reach out to him and unfold its mysteries to him.

None of that would be possible when he had to share its purity with a woman who bartered her flesh and her conscience for money—a woman who was the complete opposite of the kind of woman he admired.

But he *had* wanted her.

Briefly, foolishly, shamefully, and in a moment of lost self-control. It would not happen again.

She would never have agreed to this trip if she had known they were going to be alone, Sam fumed. He should have told her and given her the opportunity to refuse. But of course he was far too arrogant to do anything like that. So far as he was concerned his word was law. She frowned, remembering something, turning her head to look at him as she challenged him.

'I thought no one other than desert-qualified Arab drivers were allowed to drive members of the teams? Or don't the rules apply when one is the Ruler of one's own kingdom.'

She could see anger deepening the colour of his eyes. He obviously didn't like what she was saying one little bit. Did she really want to think of herself as the kind of woman who was attracted to his kind of man? Of course she didn't, she assured herself.

'I *am* a desert-qualified driver,' he told her coldly, looking away from her to switch on the car's satellite navigation and communication system, and using the earpiece he had put on to say something in Arabic to the camp's radio controller, effectively making it impossible for Sam to rally and make a retort.

Good—she was glad that he was making it plain that he didn't want to talk to her, because she certainly did not want to talk to him! In fact she didn't want any kind of contact with him at all!

The four-by-four might be the most comfortable vehicle she had ever travelled in, with its air conditioning and its leather seats that could be electronically contoured to fit one's own body for maximum support, but she certainly wasn't going to be able to relax enough to enjoy that comfort, Sam admitted. And not just because of the number of steep sand dune escarpments they were having to climb and then descend as the Prince took what she could only assume must be a shortcut to their destination.

There was also the fact that tonight they would be sharing a camp. Not, of course, that she had anything to fear from him. She knew that. And she had made overnight stays with other members of the team—it was part and parcel of their work, after all, and taken as such by everyone concerned. Anne hadn't even blinked when Sam had told her about this trip, for instance.

Other members of the team, Sam reminded herself. Never just one person…just one man…*this* man…to whom, no matter how hard she might try to deny it to herself, she was dangerously vulnerable.

Not any more! That had been before, when she had thought both of them were caught up in the same surge of mutual unstoppable passion that was beyond their control, when she had believed that they shared something very intimate and special, however out of character for her it had been. Then, of course, the thought of a night alone with him under the stars with only the desert and the night sky to witness their being together would have been her idea of heaven. Desert nights were cold—cold enough for two people who desired one another to positively need to share the heat of their bodies and their desire.

Sam couldn't think of anywhere more perfect than the desert, with all its powerful secrets, under the moon, with all its magical mystery, to consummate a love affair between two people who shared the same desire so intimately that they almost shared the same heartbeat. The male strength of the desert tamed by the female allure of the moon had surely been created to be together for an eternity that symbolised the best of human love.

Why was she letting herself think like this when she knew she could only hurt herself by doing so? It would have been hard enough for her had he merely ignored her, indicating that he wanted to pretend that embrace in the hotel corridor had never taken place. He had gone several steps further than that, though, with his criticism and accusations against her professionalism. He wasn't just indifferent to her, he actively disliked her. And she returned that dislike now, Sam told herself firmly.

Nothing could be more hellish, surely, than for two people to be alone together when their hostility towards one another was as strong as that between the Prince and herself. He had made his loathing of her very plain, and she was honour-bound to reciprocate it.

For some reason Sam suddenly felt very close to tears, her heart as raw with pain as her throat would have been had she actually been crying.

It was pointless regretting now what couldn't be changed. All she could do was resolve to make sure in every single way she could that he had no further opportunity to throw in her face any accusation about her coming on to him sexually. That should be easy enough to do, surely? After all, she had been celibate virtually all her grown-up female life, so it wasn't as though she carried with her a fully awakened sexual lust that needed to be satisfied.

The irony of her situation was its own form of black humour. Here she was, a virgin still in the emotionally and sexually fulfilled sense. Her single experience of 'full sex' had been the fumbled and uncomfortable experience she had shared with a fellow undergraduate when she had traded her virginity for the right, as she had thought then, to call herself a woman. Being accused of attempting to seduce a man who any woman could see had at his disposal all the experience and sensuality that any woman could want in a lover was absurd.

Was that why she had succumbed to temptation so easily? Because in her heart of hearts she knew that she had deprived herself of a passionately loving journey into womanhood and secretly longed to experience its mystery? Had she looked at him and somehow believed that in his arms she could find what she had never had? It was less painful to think that than to think, as she had done initially and ridiculously, that they were fated to meet and be together.

Ridiculous, yes. But how very different things could have been if *he* had shared that shock of awareness and longing she had felt at their first touch. She would have given herself willingly—eagerly, in fact—into his hands, just for the joy of knowing the reality of true sensual pleasure and satisfaction, without asking anything from him other than his own reciprocal pleasure in their coming together. She could easily have lived off the sweetness of that remembered pleasure, storing it up inside her like the most precious of precious gifts, treasuring it and revering it for all her life as a time apart from reality, without expecting or needing anything else.

But he had not offered her that gift. Instead he had made accusations against her and humiliated her. Sam gave a small gasp of pain as her feelings pushed against the barriers she had tried to erect against them. This was definitely not the time to give in to her emotions, she warned herself.

Vere glanced towards the passenger seat. He prided himself on the excellence of his desert driving, and so far as he was aware he had done nothing to elicit the small sharp sound of pain from the woman seated next to him.

He looked at the satellite navigation system map and then checked the onboard compass. They were out of range of radio frequency now, but he had no fear of them not reaching their destination.

Vere had lied to Sam when he had told her that he knew nothing about the course of the river having been changed.

The source of the river had a deep-rooted significance for his family, and his parents had brought him and Drax here often. He and Drax had kept up the tradition, coming in the winter to camp beside the river their ancestor was supposed to have conjured up so magically from the rocks, and Vere was perfectly well aware of how and why the original course of the river had been changed. What he didn't know, though, was what interpretation Ms Sam McLellan intended to put on that change when, as the Emir's pawn, she started trying to make trouble for Dhurahn.

By the time they returned to the main camp tomorrow he would be in possession of that information, and he intended to have made sure that Sam McLellan knew that he would be merciless in destroying her credibility if he had to do so to protect his country and his people.

Sam gasped as the four-by-four suddenly seemed to surge up a slope so perpendicular that her heart was in her mouth. With every metre they climbed she held her breath, expecting at best to feel the wheels spin as they sank into the sand and at worst to find that they were sliding sideways back down the incline.

Vere seemed oblivious to her concern. In fact when she looked at him she could see that he was smiling grimly as though he was enjoying forcing the hostile terrain to accept his mastery. And then suddenly the pressure forcing her back in her seat was released as they crested the incline.

'There is our camp. We should be there in a few more minutes.'

The calm words gave no hint of the triumphant satisfaction she had sensed minutes earlier as he battled the steep hill.

Down below them Sam could see dozens of small pinpricks of light, whilst the moon revealed the outlines of two of the now familiar black Bedou tents.

Sam's eyes widened. She had assumed that they would have to make their own camp, but plainly she'd been wrong. People had obviously come out here ahead to establish the camp for them. The thought of others having to toil in the hot sun to set up this camp angered her, as well as underlining yet again the difference in their status.

'It all looks very welcoming,' she told him coolly. 'I hate to think of the waste of energy resources it must represent, though.'

Vere frowned. Dhurahn was arguably the most 'green' of all the states involved in the project. He and Drax were both committed to cutting Dhurahn's own greenhouse gases, and he didn't like Sam's coolly cynical comment.

'It's never a good idea to make assumptions—especially when one is doing so without the benefit of any real knowledge or expertise. For instance the lights you can see are solar fuelled, and water will be collected in the traditional way overnight from the change in temperature. Dhurahn is known as the greenstate of the gulf, and we take our responsibility to the environment very seriously.'

'But you drive a gas-guzzler,' Sam interrupted him, adding pointedly, 'but then of course as an Arab prince I dare say you feel it is your right.'

'Dhurahn does not have its own oil. This "gas-guzzler", as you call it, has been adapted to run in the most fuel efficient way possible. Along with our neighbours in Zuran, we are financing research into alternative eco-friendly fuels. I may be an Arab prince, Ms McLellan but I come from a people who know very well how to live alongside nature and respect it. As the Ruler of Dhurahn it is my privilege to honour the traditions of my people, rather than dishonour them by seeking to emulate the greedy consumerism that has caused so much human suffering.'

Sam opened her mouth to argue with him and then closed it again. What, after all, could she say? She had not expected him to be so fiercely determined about asserting his green credentials, and she felt slightly resentful of the way it seemed he had scored the moral high ground in having done so. How childish was that? Surely what was more important was his commitment to green issues, not her savouring a small moral victory. She had only wanted to be victorious because he kept on putting her down and making her feel small, making her feel that she had no value. But then to him she didn't, and she might as well accept that.

They had almost reached the small camp now, and Sam could see where the moon was reflected on a small pool of water beneath a rocky outcrop. She remembered seeing it when she had come out originally to look at the river. She had thought then that it was a beautiful spot, with vegetation around the pool framing it in a lush green halo, the rocks so old and worn smooth by time, that she had felt a sense of awe just looking at them. The privilege of seeing such beauty softened her mood, allowing her earlier irritation to slip from her. How could anyone not marvel at something like this? This was the reason she had wanted this posting—this miracle that was the desert when it bloomed.

'The spring for the pool must be underground,' she heard herself saying softly.

Vere looked at her. A look of shining reverence illuminated her face, and like the soft awe in her voice, it caught him off guard. As though a barrier within him had been removed, he could feel the swift flood of his own longing swirling powerfully through him. He wanted her! Angry denial gripped his insides, but the truth couldn't be ignored. Against everything he knew to be in his own best interests, and more importantly those of his people, he *did* want her.

He turned away from her. As a boy, he too had marvelled at the pool, thinking it magical, whereas Drax, as always more practically minded than him, had wanted to dive down and find out where the spring actually was.

'You will do no such thing,' their father had told them both sternly. 'It is far too dangerous. Besides, I can tell you that the spring is situated beneath the rocks. It ebbs and flows in a way known only to itself, but with a pull that is dangerously strong.'

Like the pull of this woman, whose presence he resented so much, on the desire within him that he could not subjugate to his will? How swiftly and treacherously that knowledge slid into his consciousness—the merest dart of awareness, yet as powerful as any narcotic and surely as compulsive, stealing away the mind's strength whilst feeding the heart's desire. It was, he knew, no matter how much he wished he did not have that knowledge, a pull that was capable of changing the course of his life for ever if he did not control it.

Vere's hands tightened on the steering wheel of the four-by-four, and then, with an abruptness that made Sam's body recoil against the sudden acceleration of the vehicle, he drove towards their camp.

CHAPTER SIX

COMFORTABLY settled in the privacy of her own tent, Sam reflected that whilst it had disconcerted her at first to discover that the two of them were to be the only occupants of the well-organised camp, there were also certain benefits to be found. Its quiet solitude after the busy hum of the main camp was blissful, Sam thought, at least to someone like her, who valued her privacy.

Here, she knew that she was unlikely to be disturbed by a fellow worker wanting company. Deep down inside Sam knew that she felt slightly cheated and disappointed by the everyday activities of the main camp. But she knew it was silly and almost childish of her to have imagined that she would be experiencing true life in the desert, as lived by its nomads, and she had to admit she welcomed the camp's modern comforts.

The Prince had left her with the curt instruction that he expected her to be ready at first light to drive out with him to the place where she claimed the course of the river had been altered, which meant that she ought now to be in bed and asleep, ready for an early start, instead of sitting cross-legged on a cushion on the carpeted floor of her tent, wearing the thin cotton robe she had put on after her shower, her computer switched on in front of her.

Ostensibly she was checking her facts with regard to the original course of the river and answering her e-mails, but she hadn't been able to resist the temptation to bring up the now familiar details of Dhurahn and its ruling family from her previous searches.

It wasn't really the foolish self-indulgence of a woman helplessly caught in the invisible web of one man's sexual aura that was driving her, she assured herself. Naturally she was curious about the background of a man who was behaving towards her with the kind of arrogance the Prince was.

Her breath caught in her throat as she suddenly found a new site, her whole attention focused on the screen as she learned from it what she had not realised before. Namely that he, the Ruler of Dhurahn, Prince Vereham al a' Karim bin Hakar, was the elder of a pair of twins. There were two of them? Surely it wasn't possible that the world could accommodate two such men, never mind one small country.

The site gave a few more details about them, including the information that their Bedouin ancestry was mixed with the French and Irish genes of their great-grandmother and their mother.

She frowned slightly as she read these facts. How did a man who obviously had such a strong commitment to his Arab heritage deal with such a potentially turbulent mixture of cultures within himself? Did it make him resent the cultural diversity within him or embrace it? Was he at war with that inheritance or at peace with it? And what kind of woman would most appeal to a man so complex?

He would father beautiful children.

A slow, hot ache slid through her body—a need that was surely elemental and universal, the need of a woman to bear the child of a man. Not any man, but *the* man.

Panic and denial shot through her. Now look what she had done! The computer, like a modern magical vessel of legend, had released genii in the shape of knowledge conjured up by her own thoughts, and it was too powerful for her to control.

Motherhood was something she had hoped to look forward to when eventually she met the man with whom she wanted to share her life, but it had certainly never dominated her thoughts or been a desire that drove her. Yet here she was thinking in terms of having *his* child, feeling her womb tighten with longing for that child and for him. What did that tell her?

Sam sat back from the computer, feeling slightly sick as the reality of exactly what it did mean was forced on her. There was only one reason she could ever want to conceive a specific man's child as powerfully as she did this man's.

She wanted his child because she had fallen head over heels in love with him. She started to panic. No. That wasn't possible. It *shouldn't* be possible. But somehow it certainly was.

This was crazy. It just wasn't logical to fall in love with someone on the strength of a single look followed by a single kiss—especially when that someone had made it clear that he had felt nothing for her other than dislike and contempt.

Crazy or not, it was what had happened to her, so

she'd better get used to it and then work on some way of dealing with it.

Like what? Running away? Lying to herself and telling herself that she'd got it wrong, that she didn't really love him at all?

Why had this happened to her? She just wasn't the type. She was sensible, practical, she'd never believed in falling in love at first sight. She'd believed that love was something that should grow slowly and cautiously, as two people got to know one another. Love meant liking a person, respecting them and sharing goals with them. It meant…..

It meant that she had known nothing about love at all, and now that she did she wished desperately that she hadn't found out.

It was gone midnight. Vere looked up from the maps he had been studying, forwarded to him in an e-mail attachment by Drax. The earlier dated map was the original one, drawn in the days when, after the end of the First World War the Ottoman Empire had originally been carved up. The map had been handed to his great-grandfather at the same time as he had been stealing the heart of another British diplomat's daughter. It showed the boundaries between all the Arab states, including their own. It also showed the original course of the Dhurhani River. Alongside it Vere had placed the second map, dated only a matter of months later, showing exactly the same boundaries but with the river diverted to a new course. In both maps the course of the river was well within their own border.

However, the Emir, being the wily manipulator that he

was, would, Vere knew, use this alteration from the original to stir up trouble for them if he could, by hinting that if one supposedly innocent change had been made, and never revealed, what was to stop another, less innocent change being made and kept hidden.

How much had he paid Sam McLellan? However much it had been, the Emir would no doubt think he had got a real bargain. Vere had few doubts that initially all the Emir had hoped for at the very best would be to bribe the cartographer into dropping hints that the original borders had been tampered with. That would have been easy enough for her to do, given the changes that so many years of shifting desert sands had had on the landscape. But with the right kind of spin on it any change could quite easily be promoted as suspicious and underhand. Even if the allegation was retracted at a later date, the damage would have been done and Dhurahn's own reputation tarnished.

This matter of the change in course of the river put a whole new complexion on everything, and would add far more weight to any claim the Emir chose to make.

It would be easy enough for them to offer Sam more than the Emir had paid her, to 'forget' what she had discovered, but he and Drax had talked it over and they were both agreed that this was something they did not want to do. For one thing it ultimately weakened their truthful claim that the course of the river had had no effect whatsoever on their boundaries, and for another that was not the way they wanted to run their country.

Vere stood up and walked to the exit to his tent, stepping through it to breathe in the cool freshness of the night air. He stopped when he saw that there was a light on in Sam's tent.

What was she doing? Surely she ought to be asleep? He had already told her they had an early start in the morning. Could she have gone to bed and left her lamp on? Old habits died hard, and Vere and Drax's father had taught them when they were very young about the dangers of unattended oil lamps left in tents. Even though logically there was no need for him to be concerned, since a small generator was providing them with electricity, Vere was soon striding over to Sam's tent and flicking back the flap.

Once he had done so, the sight of Sam seated with her back to him, staring into a computer screen, had him walking towards her.

This time Sam was oblivious to his presence. She was staring at the screen without really seeing it as she battled against the reality being forced on her. She couldn't love him. It was—

The shadow falling across her computer screen made her react immediately and instinctively, turning round in alarm. The colour left her face and then returned in a surge of guilty heat as she tried to reach for her mouse to close the open window before showing what she had been viewing.

Vere was too quick for her, though, reaching out to stop her, his fingers curling round her wrist, the cool white crispness of his sleeve brushing against her. She saw that he had removed the plain white headdress he wore, secured by a black plaited rope, and that his hair beneath it was thick and dark, clean with health, and cut close into his neck at the back. She had an absurd longing to reach out and trace the line where it was cut so neatly against the strong muscles of his neck, and then to trace kisses along his collarbone whilst…

Frantically she wrenched her thoughts away from the sensual images forming inside her head and tried to focus instead on the grimness of the tight line around his mouth, rather than the shape of his mouth itself as he studied the information on her screen.

Sam's face burned as she realised that she had actually highlighted his own name.

'Why?' he demanded, after giving the screen a comprehensive look.

Sam understood perfectly well what he was asking her.

'I wanted to…to know now more about you…to understand why you are behaving towards me in the way that you are,' she answered him bravely. 'I didn't even know your full name.'

He looked back at the screen, indicating where she had highlighted his name and title.

'And you believe you have found it there?'

Sam was confused.

'What do you mean?'

'Those are my formal names. Vere is the name those closest to me know me by. It was my mother's choice—' Vere stopped sharply.

What was he doing? What had got into him? Why was he letting himself imagine how her lips might form the shortened version of his name, how her tongue-tip might taste, how it might sigh against his skin in a soft sound of pleasure.

'Vere,' Sam said, gasping a little when he released her wrist and then took the mouse from her to close down the site so fiercely that she started to overbalance.

As she struggled to stop herself from falling Vere moved faster, grasping her upper arms and hauling her to her feet. He was breathing rapidly, his fingers biting into her flesh. Sam thought that he might have cursed her under his breath, but she couldn't hear anything above the frantic pounding of her own heartbeat. She could smell the heat of his flesh and of their shared tension. It closed in around them, an invisible net of arousal and need meshing so tightly together that it was impossible to break free.

'No…' Sam heard the sound her lips had framed, but it was more a low moan of longing than any kind of denial, and the hands she had lifted to his chest weren't pushing him away.

'A thousand curses on you for doing this, and on me for wanting it,' Vere whispered harshly against her mouth, as she opened it for him with the inbuilt sensual knowledge of a woman who loved a man whose pride could only be humbled by his own need.

Feverishly their lips met and parted, only to meet again and again, until they were pressed body to body. Somehow Sam realised she had managed to open the buttons securing the front of his *kandora*, and her palms were now pressed flat against his chest. Her own robe had slipped from one shoulder, revealing the silky gleam of her pale skin and the curve of her breast, and the fabric was only kept from sliding down further because Vere's hand was on her, shaping the soft female texture of her flesh.

Her sensory receptors had gone into overload, her body

a melting, swirling, frenzied mass of longing. A hundred thousand separate and acutely intense sensations filled her.

Now she could fulfil that earlier urge to touch her fingertips to his skin in awed delight and wonder. She pressed them against his collarbone. His flesh felt warm and sleek, the bone beneath it hard and solid, and her gaze fastened on the spasmodic pulse jerking against the flesh just beneath his jaw. Tenderly she kissed it, lost in her own loving pleasure before being flung tumultuously into sharp, agonised passion when he responded in kind, kissing her throat and then her shoulder. A swift shudder of pleasure flowed through her at the touch of his hand freeing her breast from its covering, followed by another that racked her more visibly when his palm took the weight of it and the pad of his thumb rubbed erotically over her eagerly swollen nipple.

By the time they kissed their way to her bed both of them were naked, and Sam's body was so erotically charged by the touch of Vere's hands that she was already engulfed by fierce shivers of pleasure.

The lamp was still on, casting its illumination over their bodies, causing Sam to suck in her breath when the movement Vere made to lift her away from himself and onto the bed revealed in clear detail every strongly muscled line of him to her. His flesh was warmly golden, and his chest was sleek with fine dark hair that made an erotic pathway down his body, drawing her eager gaze to the stiff thickness of his erection.

Was love always like this? she wondered dizzily. Did every woman who fell in love feel this mixture of tenderness and awe, this desire to see and touch and taste this male uniqueness? To feel this surge of need to know that no other woman would ever share his intimacy?

She was looking at him as every man wanted the woman he desired to look at him, Vere acknowledged, as he fought against the surging heat of his physical response to her. She was looking at him as though she had just seen the world's rarest and best treasure.

She was a very good actress, that was all, he warned. But his body wasn't listening to him and it was too late now to make it listen. Her skin was the colour of milk, spread against the soft coffee colour of the bedding. The honey blonde curls on her head were matched by those that nestled against her sex, providing a covering that served more to draw attention to the soft flesh beneath than conceal it. He lifted his hand and laid it over her sex, cupping it and feeling the heavy kick of heat that punched through him as she arched upwards. Her nipples were flushed a dark rose colour against her paleness, and when he softly pinched one of them she cried out in longing, and gripped his shoulders as she urged him down to her.

He could feel the bite of her nails against his skin like a goad, the slight pain they were inflicting underlining and enhancing the ferocity of his own passion. Like a dam newly breached it surged and boiled, flooding through him to sweep aside anything and everything that tried to stand in its way. It knew no master other than itself, and it dictated where it placed his lips, his hands, and the words of encouragement and enticement he whispered so passionately.

He tasted of musk and sweat, sharpened with salt where the cool night air touched the warm, nude male flesh that wasn't heated by her own body, and Sam knew that his scent would be with her for ever, just like every precious breath of time they were now sharing.

All the reasons she should not be doing this had been left behind, abandoned and unwanted. In the lamplight she could see the small indentations left on his skin by her nails. The sight filled her with an almost primitive surge of female triumph. He was hers now, his flesh bearing her mark of possession just as all the places of sensuality on her were receiving the brand of his touch.

He was bending his head, running his tongue over her nipples, first one and then the other. Both were now swollen and tight, gleaming damply from his caress.

He covered one with his mouth and tugged delicately on it, causing a burst of violent pleasure to galvanise her whole body as she felt the soft, deliriously erotic grate of his teeth against her sensitive flesh.

She must have cried out, because she could hear the echo of her longing shuddering round the tent. His every touch was a dizzying new pleasure previously unknown to her and unexplored. Nothing in that youthful fumble long ago had prepared her for this. It was all so new, like stumbling upon an unsuspected secret hoard of priceless treasure. She wanted to linger over every individual piece, taking her pleasure in it and from it, but at the same time she was being driven by an ever-increasing sense of urgency that would not rest.

Vere could feel the thundering jolt of his heart slamming into his chest. Why was he reacting like this? Like a boy with his first woman—all trembling hands and pounding heart, half afraid that his body was so out of control that he might end up disappointing her and shaming himself. The ability to be a considerate and accomplished lover was a skill he had set himself the task of learning as part of his journey along the road to manhood, along with many other things. His goal had been to gain that skill, not to take pleasure for himself, and now he was being overwhelmed by needs and sensations that were totally new to him.

He wanted her so badly. More than he had ever wanted anything or anyone. He wanted her, bone and soul deep, burned into him and branded on him in such a way that she would forever be a part of him. Like a fever, even when the desire left him it would be inside him, and he was powerless to stop that.

He reached out to cup her sex with his hand, his fingers trembling slightly as she yielded to his caress.

Sam moaned, her body trembling beneath the intensity of her need. She curled her fingers into her palms, silently willing him to touch her more intimately, and then realising when he did that even that was not enough to satisfy the hunger gnawing at her.

She was so soft, so wet, and his body wanted her so badly. *He* wanted her so badly, Vere admitted. And that need pushed aside all the barriers he had shored up against that admission and the full extent of his own subjugation to it swept over him. He had tried to avoid this, had even tried to stop it, but now, in a final moment of true knowledge of himself and his fate, Vere was face to face with the truth, heart to heart with the woman who had brought him to it, and there was no going back.

Vere positioned himself over her, unable to deny himself the pleasure of caressing her as he prepared to enter her. Her body welcomed him and embraced him so sweetly that it was like coming home to a place that was his and his alone. Each stroke, each thrust of their bodies as they came together, was a perfect meeting of two halves of one whole. This was his fate and he welcomed it.

This was it—this was what she had yearned and ached for, what she had been made for. Sam shivered with excitement as she felt each firm thrust of Vere's body within her own. How could anything be so perfect, so uplifting and emotionally intense that it filled her eyes with tears and made her throat ache with the sounds of her own joy? She could feel every movement of him within her, every particle of him, as though her own flesh was so extraordinarily sensitive to his that she was aware of even the smallest pressure of male muscle against the female flesh that contained him. It had been so long that this might as well have been her first time. But of course it was not. Then she had—

Sam tensed, horrified, as she suddenly remembered what neither of them had done and ought to have done.

'Stop!' she told Vere urgently.

He hadn't heard her, Sam recognised. He was so lost in his own desire and in her own... She struggled to do what her conscience was urging her to do, but it was far too late. She was as powerless as he was to resist the swift tide of ecstasy he was driving her to ride. If she had to stop now... But she couldn't. Instead she clung to him as she cried out when the pleasure became too intense and took her to the stars, then gasped and wept tears of joy whilst the final pulse of the satisfaction he had given her met the forceful surge of his completion.

The heat of their mutual desire had cooled now, and yet Vere was still here with her, still holding her—surely in a parody of the tenderness she secretly longed for and knew she could not expect. It was lust that had driven him to have sex with her, that was all. How could it possibly be anything else after the things he had said to her and the way he had behaved towards her?

He should go. Vere knew that—just as he knew he should never have come here in the first place. Had a part of him realised even before they had left the main camp that this would happen? Had he deliberately planned for this? He had certainly wanted it—and her. Everything about their coming together had been wrong, and yet everything about it and her had felt so very right—more right than he could ever possibly have imagined sexual intimacy to be for him. Lying here now, with her in his arms, for the first time since the death of his parents he felt at peace and complete.

What was this? He wasn't the kind of man who needed a woman to make him feel complete. He was the ruler of a small and vulnerable state: a man whose energies were needed to keep the delicate balance of power they shared with their neighbours.

Maybe so, but he was also a man, and right now all he wanted was to be that man and be with this woman. This woman who was causing him so much trouble—a woman who had been bought by another man. Vere knew that he should reject her and leave her, but somehow he couldn't. His emotional need to be with her surmounted what his head was telling him to do.

He lifted his hand to cup her face, feeling his heart turn over inside his chest when she turned her head to press a small fierce kiss into his palm. It was as though the sexual release of their lovemaking had opened a door into his emotions, allowing them to spill out from the place where he had locked them away. He had wanted her like this from that first heartbeat of recognition, that first look and touch. It was too late now to deny it. Something about her compelled and commanded him, overturning every barrier between them.

Sam looked at Vere with helpless adoration. He was being so tender, so very much the lover she had dreamed he would be from that first moment of seeing him. The awkward experience that had dealt with her physical virginity had done nothing to change the status of her emotional and sexual virginity—that was something she had only experienced now, in Vere's arms.

Sam knew without him having to say so that Vere wanted them to make love again—but she had no excuse this time. The practicalities had to be discussed and dealt with.

'No,' she told him gently, staying his hand as it moved down her body.

Immediately Vere withdrew slightly from her, the old wariness taking the place of his earlier mood. She was rejecting him, pushing him away, and he could feel the pain he had always dreaded tightening its grip on his heart.

'No?' he queried sharply.

'We shouldn't have done what we did the first time without taking proper precautions,' Sam told him.

'Precautions?'

Vere was looking at her as though she were speaking a foreign language, Sam thought.

'I'm not using any form of birth control,' she told him quietly. 'And then there's the matter of our mutual sexual health. I.... My last partner was my first, and that was a long time ago, so I know there is no question of me being a risk to you....' She was stumbling a little over her words now, self-conscious in the reality they were creating in a way she hadn't been during their physical intimacy.

Vere registered the surge of male pleasure it gave him to hear her hesitant admission about her lack of any real kind of sexual history, but it was pushed slightly to one side by his outrage that she should find it necessary to question his own sexual morality and healthiness.

Vere looked so affronted that had it not been for the seriousness of the situation Sam could almost have laughed.

'You cannot imagine that my sexual health could in any way put you at risk,' he challenged her.

'Why not?' Sam countered steadily. 'You're a sexually active man, after all.' Her voice might have sounded steady, but she was glad to be able to duck her head so that he couldn't look into her eyes and see there the pain it caused her to think of him with other women.

'How do you deduce that?' Vere demanded peremptorily. 'Since, by your own admission, I am only the second man you have given yourself to.'

'A man in your position is bound to...to have experienced more of life in every way than a woman in mine,' Sam answered him and then added huskily, 'besides, I cannot imagine that a man could...'

'Could what?' Vere demanded, when she suddenly went silent and refused to look at him.

'Could make love to a woman as beautifully as you made love to me without...without having a lot of previous experience,' Sam said reluctantly.

Somehow or other he had reached for her hand, was holding it tightly in his own.

'If the experience was beautiful then that was because of the uniqueness of what you brought to it yourself.'

Vere hesitated. He wanted to tell her how much her soft and honest words meant to him. He want to tell her too that he shared her feelings, but he had spent too long forcing himself to keep his emotions under control and hidden, sometimes even from himself.

'I assure you that there is no risk to your health from the intimacy we have shared,' he told her briefly instead, then hesitated before adding, 'however, as to the risk of you conceiving my child…'

If she hadn't known how she felt about him before, she must know now. On hearing him say those words, at the thought of having his child, she felt her emotions close around her heart, the pressure of them like a giant fist, making the organ thud and kick. If only she might!

Sam knew she ought to be shocked by her own reckless thoughts, but the seed of an unexpected yearning had been placed inside her, and was already swelling and growing. An unplanned pregnancy was the last thing she needed in her life. But to have this man's child…his son…to have a part of him with her for ever…

Luckily for her that was unlikely to happen, Sam realised as she did a bit of quick mental arithmetic and then told Vere lightly, 'I doubt very much that I will have conceived, given the…the timing.'

'And if you have?' Vere challenged her.

'I haven't,' Sam insisted.

Abruptly Vere released her and turned away from her,

getting up from the bed. The glow from the lamp lovingly illuminated every perfect male line of his body—but not as lovingly as she wanted to trace and kiss them with her fingers and her lips, Sam thought achingly. She didn't want him to leave her. She wanted him to stay with her and hold her, love her…

She wanted what she already knew she could not have, she warned herself as Vere reached for his clothes in silence.

Vere had no idea why Sam's assertion that she had not conceived his child should make him feel that dark bitterness and pain. All he did know was that it also made him feel angry and alone. Shamefully, it also made him feel that he wanted to take her back in his arms and make love to her until she was crying out to him to possess her. And this time when he did so he wanted to ensure that… That what? That he impregnated her with his seed? That her body, her womb, would ripen with it and with his child? The fierce clutch of savage joy at his heart was giving him a message that was totally at odds with the logical rejection inside his head.

He was Dhurahn's ruler. It was impossible for him to father a child, his first child, capriciously and outside marriage. How would he ever be able to assuage the guilt he would feel towards his people and towards that child—especially if it were a son—knowing he had deprived him of his birthright?

There must be no such child, and therefore no more unprotected sex. That meant no sex at all, since it was impossible for him to procure the protection they would need unless he made an incognito visit to Zuran.

Now he *was* being ridiculous, Vere told himself as he finished dressing and then strode towards the exit of the tent without turning round to say anything to Sam. He knew that if he did he would not be able to leave her.

He had gone and Sam was alone. Her eyes were burning with tears she was determined were not going to fall. It was all her own fault. She couldn't pretend to herself that she hadn't ached to know him as a lover because she had— from the very first moment she had bumped into him. And now she did know, she knew too that, no matter what happened in the rest of her life, no man would ever be able to take her to the heights Vere had shown her. Nor the depths of pain and despair she was now feeling because he had left her.

CHAPTER SEVEN

'AND as you can see from the shape of the natural depression here, this must originally have been a deeper pool in the riverbed. My guess is that the river must at one time have cascaded down into it over this rocky outcrop to form a natural pool before flowing on.'

They were standing in the basin, in the shadow of the rock above them. Sam knew that her voice sounded stiff and over controlled as she underlined for him just why she was so sure that the course of the river had been changed. She focused straight ahead of herself, instead of turning to look at Vere. How could she behave naturally towards him now, after last night? She had barely slept, and had been unable to eat anything before he had driven her out here just as dawn was breaking. She felt so strung out by the intensity of her own emotions that just having to breathe separately from him, when all of her was screaming to be as physically and emotionally close to him as she could get, required her total concentration.

She could feel herself shaking with need. In an attempt to conceal it she bent down and picked up a handful of smooth pebbles.

'These must have been worn smooth by the river,' she told him. 'There is no other way that could have happened. The river must once have flowed into this pool and then out of it. You can even walk along what must have been the riverbed to the marshy area where it would have joined what is now the new course of the Dhurani.'

It was obvious to Vere that she wasn't going to be persuaded that she was wrong—which meant he would need to find another way of neutralising the information she was selling to the Emir.

'We are over twenty miles from our border with Khulua, and you are talking about a change of direction in the river of a matter of a few hundred yards, if that. I fail to see what relevance it could possibly have,' he told her.

Vere's voice was clipped, and like Sam he avoided any eye contact. He had still noticed, though, how the breeze that sunrise always brought had stroked her hair, and he had been filled with a fierce, irrational need to tangle his own fingers in its silky length and bind her to him.

Her, this woman it made far more sense for him to despise rather than desire.

Last night she had given herself to him so sweetly and so completely, with such trust, that just holding her had touched and soothed sore places within himself, as though she possessed a magical ability to heal him.

No. Last night she had acted as only the most skilled of deceivers could act, and he was a fool for allowing himself to feel what he had felt.

Swiftly Vere clamped down on the argument raging inside him. He needed to think only as the Ruler of Dhurahn, and to remember the hard lesson the death of his mother had taught him. There was no place here for the man he had foolishly allowed himself to be the previous night—vulnerable, in need, responsive to a certain woman's hold on his senses to such an extent that everything else was forgotten.

Sam couldn't look at Vere. If she did... If she did, she would end up begging him to hold her, and she must not do that. She had humiliated herself enough already. Last night had shown her yet again that she meant nothing to him. If he had used her to satisfy his lust then that was her own fault, for loving him so much that she had allowed him to do so.

She had to focus on being professional. Sam took a deep breath and then said firmly, 'It must have had some relevance to whoever changed it, and it's that that fascinates me. Why would anyone want to go to the trouble of altering it, especially in view of the work it must have been involved? A new channel would have had to be cut through the rock, and that would have been expensive. To what purpose? No benefit could have been gained from it.'

'To your western mind, perhaps, but the Eastern mind thinks differently.'

Sam turned towards him, forgetting that she had promised herself she wouldn't look at him.

'So there *was* a reason?'

Her mouth looked soft and swollen still from his kisses, and the khaki shirt she was wearing couldn't conceal the aroused thrust of her nipples. Her face wore a tell-tale paleness that spoke of a night's sensual languor. The ache that was tormenting him immediately became a dervish-driven whirlwind of torture. He wanted her. He wanted to claim her now, here. He wanted— He stopped, knowing he wasn't free to feel like this, to need like this.

'Yes, there was a reason,' he agreed, forcing himself to deny the images that were tempting him. 'But it has nothing to do with protecting our right to the river, because that has never been necessary. The Dhurahni River belongs to Dhurahn. That is a legal reality that can never be changed or questioned.'

'Then why?'

Sam's persistence reactivated Vere's suspicions, and reminded him of why they were here.

It was plain to him that she was digging for information so that she could pass it on to the Emir. There was no need for him to answer her. But then neither was there any need to conceal the truth, since it was obvious that she was not going to allow herself to be persuaded that she was wrong.

Sam thought that he wasn't going to answer her. He was looking towards the rocks from where the water must once have flowed, down into the now dried-out pool in which they were standing, sheltered from the growing strength of the morning sun by the shadows cast by the rocks.

'There is a story that has been passed down through our family by word of mouth…'

The air had gone still, waiting for the sun's warmth— hungering for it, Sam guessed, in the same way that she hungered for Vere. Why had this happened to her? Why was fate subjecting her to this cruelty? Why couldn't she have loved another man? A different man? A man who might love her in return?

'When the borders between our states were originally

drawn up,' Vere continued, 'my great-grandfather claimed as his wife the daughter of a British diplomat. It is said that after their marriage my ancestor and his bride spent their first night together as man and wife here, on their journey to Dhurahn city. A camp was set up, and my great-grandfather and his bride swam together alone here—for, as you have said, this was the course of the river then. It flowed over those rocks behind us and down into a pool here.

'The story goes that the pool was one of great beauty, fringed with all manner of plants and flowers, with an olive grove beyond it. The newly married couple consummated their vows to one another here in privacy, and it was here that their first child, a son, was conceived.

'Such was my ancestor's love for his wife that he commanded that the course of the river should be diverted, so that no other man could ever look upon the pool that held within it the memories of their love and her beauty, or imagine what anyone but him had the right to know. It was their special place, and he preferred to destroy it rather than let anyone else look upon it.'

'He must have loved her very much and…and very passionately' was all that Sam could manage to say.

'Yes,' Vere agreed.

Vere watched Sam from the protection of the shadows that cloaked his own expression. Last night, in giving herself to him, she had taken a part of him he could never reclaim. He had to admit that to himself because there was no way now he could evade that knowledge.

Without him knowing quite how, she had managed to touch his carefully protected emotions. But she was not someone with whom he could ever share his life, or to whom he could ever make a commitment. No matter how much he wanted her.

How could he do that when she was in the Emir's pay? Whatever his personal feelings, his duty was to his people and their best interests. The days were gone when a man like his great-grandfather had believed it was right to put his love for a woman above all else.

His *love* for a woman?

He did not love her. He could not—would not. It was impossible, unthinkable.

When he had guarded his heart against love he had thought he was protecting it from a woman who would know him as a man, a poet—someone to whom the desert was a sacred well from which he refilled his inner being— and that it would be her knowledge of this true essence of himself that would bind them together in mutual love. She would love him *despite* the fact that he was a prince, not because of it, and she would share his belief that true honesty and trust were essential components of their love for one another. The woman would love him as his mother had loved his father—before and beyond anything or anyone else, even their children.

That woman was not this woman. He did not love this woman.

But his heart was thudding in sledgehammer-like blows, beating out a message that said he was lying to himself.

Having listened to Vere, Sam found that she was averting her gaze from the pool, not wanting to see the images Vere's story had brought to life. The young bride, her pale skin covered only by the water, and her husband, his skin darker, his body hardened by the desert and by tribal warfare, his passions aroused by his love for her. Their faces were concealed from her but their feelings were not.

To let her thoughts go further was too intrusive, and yet the images and the emotions they aroused in her couldn't be dismissed. Sam closed her eyes to shut them out, but when she opened them again the figures were still there, inside her imagination. Only now she could see their faces, and they belonged not to two unknown people but to herself and Vere. A shudder of naked longing racked her whole body.

The sun was fully risen now, its light sharpening the shadows glittering on the pebbles in the dried-out pool, now no more than an empty husk of what it had once been. It held no indication of the beauty it had known.

Vere looked at it and then looked away. His great-grand-father had loved passionately and intensely, and he had loved only one woman. To love like that was in his genes, a fate he could not avoid. But he must avoid it. He must not love this woman whom he could never trust.

Sam made a huge effort to redirect her thoughts to where they ought to be.

'If you knew the story behind the river, then why did you insist that I was wrong and that the course *hadn't* been changed?'

Her voice sounded low and strained in her own ears. She prayed that Vere wouldn't guess how difficult she was finding it to focus on what she was saying and the reason they were here.

'Why was it of so much interest to you that it had?' Vere countered, without answering her.

'Because I knew that I was *right* that it had been moved, and I knew that there had to be a reason.'

She was being very persistent. The Emir must have paid her very well indeed. So at least she had some kind of loyalty. Vere could feel the sharp acid bitterness of his own anger. It raked at his heart like wickedly sharp knives, driving him past caution.

'But of course you would have preferred that reason to be political rather than emotional?' he accused Sam bitingly.

Sam stared at him, not understanding his anger or his attack.

'Why do you say that?'

'Why do you think I say it?'

He was talking in riddles now, and Sam had no idea what they meant.

'I didn't have *any* preconceived idea about why the river had been re-routed. In fact that was part of what made it so intriguing. Logically there was no reason to move it. It isn't as though it forms part of a border, or is disputed in any way, but there had to be some motive. Everything must have a motive…'

What had been his for keeping his knowledge to himself and withholding it from her? she wondered. What had his motive been for sharing it with her now? Her instincts were warning her to be on her guard.

She was lying, of course. Vere knew it. She had to be. The only reason she had been interested in the changed course of the river was because the Emir was paying her to cause trouble for them. He knew that too.

How much had she told the Emir already? Had he, or those who had hired her on his behalf, suggested ways in which she might manipulate the facts to fit in with his personal agenda?

Had she hoped that by giving herself to him she could learn something that would aid the Emir's cause? The mere fact that he had slept with her so casually would be enough to discredit him and, via that, damage the reputation of their country. He had been a fool to let his desire for her overwhelm his judgement.

Vere thought quickly. He needed to protect Dhurahn against its current exposure to the Emir's schemes, and to negate the effect his relationship with the Emir's paid pawn might have. He needed to turn the tables on the Emir, and fast, and he thought he knew exactly how to do that.

If he were to establish Sam publicly as his official mistress, then who would place credence on any claims the Emir might try to make off the back of her investigations? No one.

Vere had no idea how such a plan had come to him. To take a person and use them without their knowledge for his ulterior purposes was ethically against everything he believed in. He wasn't doing this for himself, though, he reminded himself. He was doing it for Dhurahn.

Sam had shown herself willing to share his bed privately, so why should it make any difference to her if she shared it publicly? And their relationship would have to be shown publicly in order for it to benefit Dhurahn. The Heads of State would need to know that the 'expert witness' the Emir believed was secretly in his pocket was publicly in Vere's bed.

Publicly taking a mistress went against everything Vere held most dear, for he was a deeply private man, a man of pride and honour, but he knew that the only criticism of his actions would be his own. Drax would be more amused than shocked—all the more so if he believed that Vere genuinely felt desire for Sam—and Vere would keep from him the fact that his affair was a premeditated plan to outwit the Emir.

As for Sam herself... Vere frowned. He would make sure she was well reimbursed for her trouble, and that she knew she would be. All she needed to know was that he desired her and that he wanted her to be with him. If she was greedy and immoral enough to accept the Emir's bribe then she was hardly likely to turn down his offer, was she? A rich lover, ready to pay for the pleasure of having her in his bed, wasn't something she was going to turn her back on, was it? It was probably the kind of offer she had been hoping for from the start.

But, no matter how much he underpinned his decision with such thoughts, Vere knew that something deep inside him recoiled from it and felt tainted by it.

She had shown such trust and innocence last night, such sweetness in the way she had given herself to him so freely. Or had she? Had he simply allowed himself to think that because it was what he wanted to think? If things had been different, if *she* had been different, then his own future could have been so much happier than he had ever dreamed.

It was pointless thinking like that, Vere warned himself. He had a duty to do what must be done to protect Dhurahn.

'It's time we returned to the main camp,' he told Sam.

Sam nodded her head—but when she turned on her heel to start walking back to the four-by-four she slipped on the pebbles and lost her balance.

She could feel herself falling and cried out automatically—only to feel the breath leaking from her lungs as Vere reacted to her plight, catching hold of her and supporting her.

She looked up at him, intending only to thank him, she assured herself, but somehow her gaze slithered as helplessly to his mouth as her feet had done on the pebbles. And once there she couldn't remove it. Instead her imagination burned her senses with vivid images of a cool deep pool of water in which their naked bodies entwined as they swam together, before they stopped to stand body to body in its shallows, their hands and lips discovering one another.

'No…'

But it was too late. As though he had shared her intimate vision Vere was kissing her once, then twice, and then over and over again, as though his hunger for her was such that nothing could assuage it. Just like her hunger for him.

And when he did release her it was only to take her hand and lead her back to the four-by-four.

Neither of them spoke as he drove them back to the small camp. There was no need, Sam thought. She knew exactly what was in his mind, what he ached and yearned for, because the same thing was in her own.

In the cool shadows of her tent she watched as he undressed her, his lean long-fingered hands trembling visibly, but no more than her own fingers did when it was her turn to reach out and touch him.

Her body, knowing the delights ahead after last night, pulsed with eagerness and longing. Shrugging off the last of her clothes, she reached up to him, unable to wait any longer, urging him down towards her.

Outside the tent the sun scorched the earth in an embrace that was almost too much for it to bear. Inside, Sam lay in Vere's arms and felt that her desire for him was almost too much for her senses to bear. Several times tears scalded her eyes, and she cried out when Vere's touch carried her too close to her own pleasure.

'We mustn't,' she whispered to him. 'The risk…'

'Trust me, there will be no risk,' Vere soothed her, assuring himself that there would be no danger if he contented himself with simply pleasuring her and taking his own pleasure from that. He kissed her breasts and her belly, then moved lower, the tip of his tongue inscribing circles of indescribably intense pleasure against her thigh.

When he reached the swollen lips of her sex he stroked his fingertip along the length of its secrets. She was moist and ready, quickening to his touch, her flesh as sweet as fruit ripened to the moment of perfection. His hunger to taste her thundered through him, driving him beyond what he thought he knew of himself and what he was. It stripped away everything but his own need, forcing it and him into a single desire.

He tasted her with his tongue and then his lips. But even that wasn't enough to satisfy his need.

Unable to withstand her own pleasure, Sam cried out, her back arching and inviting. The feel of Vere sliding his body the length of hers made her sob with relief and cling to his shoulders. There was no need for her to urge him, though. He was already surging into her, filling her and completing her. He drove them both through their pleasure and beyond it to another level, and then another, each plateau more intense than the last, until finally all boundaries disappeared and they were at one with the universe, both of them oblivious to the risk they had taken.

Sam surfaced slowly through the layers of sleep that, when she had first closed her eyes, had cocooned her as securely as Vere's arms. Her body felt boneless and relaxed, and at the same time heavily sweet with the echoes of pleasure that clung to her like an invisible veil of sensation. She had never felt happier, nor more aware of how vulnerable she was. Of how finely balanced her emotions and senses were on the see saw edge of the intimacy she had shared with Vere. The heights and the depths were both there within her reach. With a single smile Vere could make her soar up to one and plunge down to the other.

Vere!

He was seated on the edge of the bed, fully dressed now, she realised, but with his head still bare. She could smell the freshly showered scent of his skin separating him from her, because her body was still perfumed with their intimacy.

'This can't be allowed to continue. For the Ruler of Dhurahn such clandestine behaviour is not fitting. Matters cannot continue as they are. Changes will have to be made.'

His harsh words plunged Sam down into the darkness of loss and despair. He was going to have her dismissed from her job, she recognised miserably.

She wanted to protest, but how could she? What could she say? No matter how much both of them might try to deny it, it was obvious that the sexual chemistry between them was too powerful for them to resist.

'I refuse to be forced to creep into your quarters under cover of darkness and then have to leave them again before the break of day, like some thief taking what he should not have. Instead I propose that you become my official mistress, and that I publicly acknowledge you as such. You will return with me to Dhurahn, where you will have your own suite of rooms in the royal palace. Your status will be recognised and respected. It is a great honour in the eyes of our people for a woman to be chosen to be their Ruler's mistress. You will share my life and my bed for as long as we continue to desire one another, and no one will dare to question our relationship.'

'You want me to be your mistress?' Sam could barely take in what he was saying, though she could feel the hollowness inside her filling with pain.

His *mistress*. How cold and unloving he made it sound—a union purely for sex, with no love or emotional bonding shared between them. There were no words from him to reassure her that, even if his position meant that he did not want to marry her, at least he cared enough to understand how important it was to her to know that he felt love for her.

'It seems a logical solution to a situation which we both know now is becoming untenable.'

She ought to turn him down and walk—no, run away from him just as far as she could, if only for the sake of her own pride. But how would she feel once she had done that? How would she feel back home in England, knowing she could have been with him? Would her pride sustain her then, when she was lying awake at night hungering for him?

It shocked her that she could feel like this, that there could even be any question of what she should do. What had happened to her inner belief that it was only within a secure and mutually committed, loving relationship that she would experience true sexual pleasure and satisfaction? What had happened to the conviction that for her a relationship without those things just wasn't worth having? That without being loved and loving in return, without being valued and valuing in return, there was no way she would want to be with a partner?

Vere offered her none of those things. Even his desire for her was a desire she felt he resented and in part blamed her for—a need which, when he wasn't being intimate with her, she suspected he felt extremely hostile towards.

Surely knowing all of these things her logic and common sense could only urge her in one direction. That direction being the opposite one from the one Vere was taking.

By rights she ought to be refusing him, telling him quite categorically that she had no wish to become his mistress. His *mistress*, she reminded herself. Not his lover. Even in choosing his wording Vere was offering her a position in his life which made them unequal.

But maybe it was understandable that he should withhold himself emotionally from her. A man in his position would have to be wary and careful. Women must throw themselves at him in their dozens. He had already accused her of doing exactly that, and said he wanted nothing more to do with her, but he had been the one who had instigated their lovemaking, and there Sam could find no fault with him at all. There, he had given her everything she had dreamed of in her wildest dreams and more.

She knew instinctively that it just wasn't possible for any other man to take her to such heights or show her such pleasures. No matter what she did from now on no one could ever match the sensuality of Vere's lovemaking. Her body would forever have desire for it and for him. Why not allow it to have what pleasure it could, even if she knew that ultimately that pleasure would be brought to an end?

She could live like that, couldn't she? She could endure the heights of sexual delight, knowing that what they had already shared had tipped her over the edge of fantasising about Vere into the painful reality of loving him, whilst Vere felt nothing emotionally for her. Was she sure she had the right degree of strength and self-discipline to separate her sexual fulfilment from the emotional barrenness of the relationship he was proposing without it destroying her?

But what if with time Vere should grow to love her? What if the sexual pleasure they shared led him to fall in love with her? Could she really bear to turn her back on the chance that that might happen?

The chance? It was a very small chance!

Yes, but it was there, wasn't it? And whilst it was there she could hope. Wasn't her love for him worth taking a risk for?

She gulped in a shallow breath of air and then exhaled, trying to steady her nerves.

'Some people might think it's an insult to a woman to offer her such a role,' she told Vere lightly.

'Might they? I doubt it. On the contrary. My opinion is that people will view the fact that I am publicly acknowledging you as a mark of my respect for you. Surely it is more insulting by far for me to be with you in secret, as though I feel that being with you shames me? As my mistress you will have status and position. Financially—'

'No!' Sam stopped him sharply. 'I don't want money to come into this. If I agree, then it is because…' she looked proudly at him. 'It is because I want you, not your money.'

'You say that, but if it is true then why do you hesitate? After all, I already know you want me.'

He had cut the ground from beneath her so neatly she had fallen straight into his trap, Sam acknowledged. She opened her mouth and then closed it again. Shaking her head, she finally admitted, 'Since you put it like that, then I don't suppose I can refuse, can I?'

'No,' Vere agreed softly. 'You can't. And nor would I have allowed you to do so.'

CHAPTER EIGHT

SAM suspected that it wasn't just the motion of the helicopter Vere had summoned to transport them swiftly to Dhurahn that was making her feel slightly dizzy. From the second she had given her agreement to Vere's proposition things had moved so fast that Sam had barely had time to catch her breath at all.

When she had protested that she needed time to explain things to her colleagues, Vere had told her arrogantly that no explanation would be needed. The very fact that she was with him would be enough. And of course he had been right.

Anne, who had come to see her whilst she had been packing, had shaken her head and taken hold of Sam's hands in hers to say, almost maternally, 'Oh, my dear, are you sure?'

'That I'm doing the right thing? No,' Sam had admitted, choking back a small laugh. 'But I'm sure that if I don't go with him I shall regret it.'

'You're in love with him,' Anne had guessed. 'Well, I can't blame you. But these men are autocrats, my dear, and their way of life…'

'I know it won't last for ever,' Sam had told her bravely.

Anne had patted her hand without reassuring her, saying only, 'I do so hope that you won't end up being hurt.'

Would she end up being hurt? Sam wondered now, as they flew over the fertile area of land irrigated by the Dhurahni river. Or would the miracle she longed for occur and Vere fall in love with her?

Down below them she could see fields of crops, olive groves, and a wide, straight arterial road.

'Our farmers grow the crops that feed the tourists who flock to Zuran,' Vere told her, leaning across her slightly, his body hard against the softness of her own.

She had already noticed the respect with which she had been treated by the men who had accompanied Vere to the camp when he had escorted her from her tent to the helicopter. She shivered a little now, still not really able to take in the public change in her circumstances. All she wanted was Vere the man, as her lover and her love, but Vere was more than Vere the man; he was also the powerful Ruler. How would she fit in to his environment?

They were flying into what Sam assumed must be Dhurahn's airport.

Sam looked uncertainly at Vere, suddenly feeling very vulnerable and anxious.

'Are you sure this is a good idea?' she asked him. 'I mean, with you being Dhurahn's Ruler…and your brother… what will he—'

'Drax will thoroughly approve.'

Sam could see how Vere's expression softened and lightened when he mentioned his twin. She felt a small pang of jealousy. Vere loved his brother. She so desperately wanted him to love her. She knew so little about Vere's life, but she felt unable to ask too many questions. What did that tell her about the imbalance in their relationship?

The helicopter had come to rest. Vere touched her arm, indicating that she was to follow him.

By the time they were standing on the concrete runway a vehicle had pulled up in front of them, the driver getting out and salaaming to Vere before opening the car doors for them.

Sam didn't know quite what she had expected. Perhaps not exactly outriders and half an army, but certainly rather more formality.

She was even more bewildered when, instead of leaving the runway, they were driven over to a waiting plane. She looked at Vere questioningly.

'We're going to Zuran,' he told her, as they were ushered out of the car and towards a waiting plane, where he stopped to say something to the pilot as Sam was escorted on board by the flight attendants.

Sam had never flown in a privately owned jet before.

'The flight time to Zuran is one hour,' the male flight attendant was telling her as he offered her a glass of champagne, which she refused. She felt giddy enough already, without drinking alcohol.

She stared round the interior of the plane, her eyes widening at the luxury of its cream carpet and blue-grey walls. Instead of rows of seats there were plush-looking leather chairs and a desk.

'If you wish to rest, there is a bedroom here,' the steward continued, opening a door and ushering her towards it. Uncertainly Sam looked inside. The bedroom was luxuriously appointed, with its own *en suite* bathroom, and it was all Sam could do not to betray just how out of her depth she was beginning to feel in the midst of so much luxury. Would Vere expect to consummate their new relationship here? Her face began to burn and her heart pumped too fast.

'Perhaps you would like something else to drink?' the steward asked

'Just water…thank you,' Sam answered and then tensed, knowing that Vere had entered the cabin even though she couldn't see him.

She turned round, her heart racing, whilst the steward made a deep obeisance. She waited for him to leave before she burst out shakily, 'I don't think I can do this. It was different in the desert, but I'm not—this…' She gestured helplessly around the cabin. 'This kind of thing…I don't think…I don't know anything about royal protocol, and even if I did that's not the way I want to live.'

'You'll get used to it,' Vere told her dismissively.

He couldn't afford for her to be having second thoughts now, and ruining his plans. Not when he was already aching for the hot sweet pleasure of holding her through the night, knowing she was his. Vere dismissed his unwelcome thoughts angrily. It was not for that reason that he was doing this.

'Dhurahn isn't Zuran,' he told Sam. 'We live relatively simply. Now, sit down and make yourself comfortable. We'll be taking off soon.'

Obediently Sam found that she was subsiding into one of the leather chairs and accepting the glass of water the steward had brought for her.

Their take-off was smooth and swift, and by the time

they had eaten the meal the steward served them they had begun their descent into Zuran.

Here, though, when they left the aircraft they were met by several important-looking officials, then ushered to a waiting limousine with blacked-out windows and a motor-cycle escort, the Zurani flag flying on its bonnet.

Sam hadn't thought to ask why they had come to Zuran, assuming it must be on some kind of state business, and she wasn't expecting it when they pulled up outside the entrance to what she knew to be Zuran's most exclusive and expensive shopping mall.

Uniformed flunkeys held open the doors for them, but when they stepped into the air-conditioned marble-floored mall it was completely empty of shoppers.

Bewildered, Sam turned to look at Vere.

'You're now my official mistress,' he told her. 'It will shame me if you are not appropriately clothed. The Ruler of Zuran has kindly offered to make the facilities of this mall available to us, so that you can be provided with all that is necessary.'

'You mean you've brought me here to buy me clothes?' Sam demanded angrily, too shocked to hide her feelings.

Vere frowned. She sounded more displeased than pleased. It was his understanding that women liked nothing better than a new designer wardrobe, and it irked him slightly that Sam was not reacting with more enthusiasm and appreciation.

'You can't have imagined that what you have will be suitable for your new role. Naturally my people will expect you to be dressed as befits that position.'

Sam wanted to tell him that she hated the thought of him

paying for her clothes because it demeaned and hurt her, it turned her into an object—the appropriately dressed mistress—but a stunningly beautifully dressed young woman was coming towards them, making any further private conversation impossible.

'Highness,' she greeted Vere respectfully, before turning to Sam. 'I am to be your personal dresser, madam. If you would like to come this way, we have arranged a private room for you in which you can relax whilst clothes are brought for your inspection.'

At last it was over.

Sam refused to look at Vere as a team of sales assistants wrapped her new clothes in tissue paper. Her eyes felt dry, burning with the shamed tears she refused to let herself cry.

The clothes Vere had bought for her *were* beautiful—exquisite Chanel suits and tops, Jimmy Choo shoes, Vera Wang evening wear, and so much more, all of it designer label and all of it earning only a brief nod of the head from Vere after she had been dressed in them and then paraded in front of him.

With each successive humiliating nod of his head Sam had felt her outrage give way to misery, until her misery had been overtaken by what she felt now. The bleak certainty that she couldn't do this.

Vere frowned as he watched Sam's reaction to the growing pile of shiny bags and boxes. The more the quantity grew, the more she seemed to withdraw into herself—so much so that she was actually physically stepping back from the garments and from him. Her normal warmly vivacious expression had been replaced with blank withdrawal as she focused her gaze away from both her new clothes and him.

Vere might never have been responsible for providing a woman with a brand-new designer wardrobe before, but even without that experience he knew enough to recognise that this was not the reaction he might have expected.

Half a dozen men dressed in livery that wouldn't have disgraced a Hollywood extravaganza representing the court of an *Arabian Nights* Caliph had been summoned to carry Sam's new clothes. And it would take a fleet of limousines to ferry everything to the airport, Sam reflected bleakly, forcing herself to smile at the girls who had served her. After all, it wasn't their fault that she felt the way she did. It was her own.

She had been so naïve, never envisaging anything like this when she had let her heart rule her head and agreed to enter into this relationship with Vere. She was now beginning to recognise she would not be able to endure it. She didn't want to be his mistress, with all that that implied, she wanted to be his lover… No, that wasn't true, was it? What she really wanted, she acknowledged wretchedly, was to be his love, as he was hers. But she had already told herself that that was impossible. She had already said to herself that she accepted the limitations of what he was offering her and that she could live with them. Was she now saying that she had changed her mind and she couldn't?

Tears were burning her eyes behind the protection of her sunglasses. She felt so very alone. Her parents, living in their neat detached house in a London suburb, would never understand any of this.

She hesitated in mid-step and, as though he sensed her

desire to flee, Vere reached out and took hold of her hand. He continued to hold it until they had reached the waiting limousine.

They got into it in mutual silence, and the first thing Vere did once they were inside it was close the partition that separated them from the driver, ensuring they could speak without being overheard.

'I can't do this,' Sam burst out as soon as Vere had closed the screen.

Vere's mouth compressed. 'You have already agreed.'

'That was when I thought….before…'

'Before what? Nothing has changed.'

'Of course it has. Have you any idea how humiliating it was to parade in front of you in those clothes, knowing that you would be paying for them, knowing that because I'm your mistress everyone will assume that you are paying me for sex.'

'That is often the assumption when a man takes a mistress.'

'That depends on how you define the word "mistress". I assumed that what you meant was that you wanted us to be lovers. Everything was so different when we were in the desert. There we were just two people who…who wanted one another. I love the desert. There's something so pure and pared-down about it. It makes you confront things about yourself—' Sam broke off and shook her head. 'Everything seemed so right there. Just the two of us and the desert. Nothing more. That's all I want from you, Vere. The right to be with you because it's what we both want. I don't want to be dressed up like…like an expensively wrapped trophy….'

Vere could hear the pain in her voice. It touched a place within him that he had thought protected from any touch. The desert stripped away the folly of consumerism and status and reduced a man to blood and bone and flesh. It demanded that a man meet it with only that. One either loved the desert or one feared it. Vere loved it.

He could feel the echo of Sam's emotional words striking a chord within him. It pierced the hard, protective wall he had built around his own emotions. Unwanted, dangerous thoughts and feelings pressed against that barrier, threatening it, fuelling Vere's anger against the woman who had caused them.

'It is too late to change your mind now,' he told her.

He knew that news of their shopping trip would reach the ears of the Emir, and that it would add substance to the fiction he wanted to create that Sam was indeed his mistress.

Ignoring the glossy magazines that had appeared in the jet's cabin whilst they had been in the shopping mall, Sam picked up the paperback she had bought for herself instead.

She had no idea where all the new clothes were, nor did she care. She felt weighed down with her own despair.

When Vere had asked her to be his official mistress she had envisaged long hours of sexual intimacy—not shopping trips followed by Vere involving himself in paperwork without so much as attempting to even kiss her. Admittedly the bedroom of his private jet couldn't provide the privacy she would have preferred, but if he really wanted her surely he would have managed to find same excuse to draw her in there to hold her and kiss her? He must know how alien and overwhelming she was finding all of this. After all, there couldn't be many young women in her position who wouldn't have been feeling the same.

Vere's mobile rang, showing the private number that belonged to his twin.

When he stood up and turned his back to her to take his call, Sam guessed that it must be personal and got up herself, heading for the bedroom cabin to give Vere privacy in which to take the call.

'Drax,' Vere welcomed his twin.

'I'm just about to leave for the Alliance of Arabic-Speaking Nations finance conference, but I thought I'd better let you know that the reports have come through from our agents on your Miss McLellan.'

Vere was on the point of denying that Sam was 'his', when he realised that it was hardly true any more. He needed to bring Drax up to speed with his decision.

However, before he could do so, Drax was continuing. 'We've drawn a blank, I'm afraid. Whoever it is who is in the Emir's pay it is definitely not Samantha McLellan. Our people have been over her life and her finances in microscopic detail, and there is nothing that can tie her into the Emir in any kind of way. Interestingly, though, they did discover that her computer has been hacked into whilst she's been working in the field, and their feeling is that someone has been very interested in her work.'

Sam was not in the Emir's pay.

Outrunning his shock was a wave of emotion that kicked away his defences. Now he had nothing to shield him from what she was doing to him. No way of protecting himself from the way she made him feel.

Vere struggled to wrest control from these sensations and focus on practical issues, regain some control.

'She raised the queries about the Dhurahni River being re-routed,' he managed to tell his twin. 'It could be that whoever is working for the Emir got to hear about them and thought there might be something there the Emir could use.'

'We'd better have her colleagues checked out, then,' Drax suggested.

'Yes,' Vere agreed. 'When do you expect to be back in Dhurahn?'

'I'm not sure. I've sent Sadie home ahead of me, so I don't intend to linger. She's got several weeks to go yet before the baby is due, of course, but much as I shall miss her she needs to rest—even though she insists she would rather be with me.'

'Drax?'

'Yes?'

'I'm on my way back to Dhurahn now, and I'm taking Samantha McLellan with me. It's a long story,' Vere added quickly, 'but—'

'Ah, you need say no more, brother.' Drax was laughing before Vere could tell him why he had planned to have Sam accompany him. 'I have been there myself, remember? I can tell from your voice what is happening… If you are having trouble persuading her to marry you, then…' Drax's voice faded, and then the connection was broken.

There was no point in trying to phone Drax back, Vere acknowledged. What, after all, could he say? Drax had obviously got hold of the wrong idea. Like everyone in love, Drax automatically assumed that everyone else wanted to share his exalted state. Besides, for once in his life Vere had something more important to think about than what his brother might think.

Sam was completely innocent of any wrong-doing.

The agents they employed were far too good at their job to make any mistakes, and Vere didn't even think of disputing what Drax had told him. So now he didn't need her as his mistress at all. There was no point in him establishing her in that role since she was not in the Emir's pay.

A mixture of emotions twisted through him. Fear, anger, hostility, all bound together by the ties linking him to his past and the loss of his mother. And joy, tenderness and guilt for misjudging her, woven like a gentle chain around his heart.

Out of habit, it was the older, darker emotions he allowed to claim him. They were the emotions he felt safe with. They did not require him to do anything other than go on believing as he had done for so long. They did not require a blind leap of faith. All they required and demanded was that he dismissed Sam from his life immediately.

It would be easy enough for him to tell her that he had changed his mind, and it would be a simple exercise for him to arrange for her to be taken back to the camp where she could resume her work. After all, there was no rational reason now to keep her with him, was there?

Immediately his emotions rejected the thought of letting her go. A sharp, unwanted stab of anguish pierced his heart at the thought of not having her in his life. His heart was hammering against his ribs and his whole body was tensed in rejection of the thought of losing her, whilst a battle raged within him between his need to protect himself and the desire Sam aroused within him.

He couldn't send her back, even if he wanted to, he reasoned to himself. The cartographer's position she had vacated had already been filled, and anyway, he could hardly expect her to simply carry on working at the camp as though nothing had happened. Those working with her were bound to ask questions. He surely had a duty to protect her from that.

But if he hadn't misjudged her in the first place... Though he'd had no option but to suspect her, given the circumstances, Vere defended himself.

And no option but to make love with her? His heart slammed into his ribs.

No, he had had no option there either—but for very different reasons.

He wasn't proud of what he had done, or of his own weakness, but it was for her sake and not his own that he intended to keep her with him in Dhurahn whilst he formulated some satisfactory way of compensating her for the damage his suspicions might have done to her career, as he now considered himself honour-bound to do.

And was that the only reason? Were his motives purely altruistic, and nothing whatsoever to do with his own feelings, his own desires?

She would be housed in her own quarters, and he would not intrude on those. He would find some way to ensure that her presence in Dhurahn was recognised as the professional visit of a qualified cartographer. The mouth of the Dhurahni where it reached the sea had never been properly mapped; silting had changed the course of river there. Mapping the coastline would be a very worthwhile project, and would surely go some way to redressing the harm he could have done her.

But he had already advertised the fact that she was his mistress.

She could be his lover *and* work professionally in Dhurahn. That way he could both make amends and keep her close to him. Close enough for them to…

To what?

That wasn't a question Vere could allow himself to answer.

She had told him, though, that she had changed her mind and no longer wanted to go with him. If he had any sense he would accept that and let her go.

But within a heartbeat he was reminding himself that she had only changed her mind about the outward image of her role, not about the inner, intimate living of it. She had said herself that she wanted him.

A hot surge of male need speared through him. They were already lovers. Would it really be so wrong for them to continue to be so? No one, least of all his twin, would deny him the right to set aside the responsibilities of rulership and simply be a man. And by needing her he was not really allowing himself to become vulnerable. Needing wasn't loving. He could need her without loving her. He did not love her. He would not love her. So there was really no reason why she should not stay, was there? Unless, of course, he secretly thought that he was in danger of loving her?

Of course he wasn't.

Sam had put as much distance as she could between herself and Vere, neither looking at him nor talking to him during the flight.

A group of officials were waiting to greet Vere as they left the jet. Sam deliberately kept herself in the shadows, which was surely the correct place for a mistress—especially one dressed like her, in the same serviceable clothes she had taken with her to the desert. But even if she had been able to bring herself to change into any of the new clothes Vere had bought her she would still have hung back, Sam knew.

She caught one of the officials, a young woman with dark eyes that flashed liquid with longing whenever she looked at Vere, staring at her. Unlike her, the woman was standing tall with pride and self-respect, her sunglasses perched on her head, all the better for Vere to admire those magnificent tawny eyes of hers, Sam reflected miserably, and the equally magnificent cleavage just teasingly hinted at by the V in her crisp tailored shirt.

Why had she agreed to this? Sam asked herself wretchedly. It was obvious to her that she had been a fool to think that Vere could ever come to love her. She had allowed herself to be carried away by her own longing and the romance of the desert, where they had just been two people unable to fight a mutual desire for one another. That, however, had merely been a desert mirage, that was all. The reality was what was here in front of her now. And that reality wasn't a man she had deceived herself into creating out of her own need, a man she could reach out to and connect with, if only via his desire for her.

The reality was this stranger, dressed now not simply, as she had seen him in the desert, but wearing over his plain white *dishdasha* a rich dark blue silk robe embroidered with gold thread, which he had put on before they left the aircraft. There might not be a crown on his head, but it might just as well be there. Both his manner and that of those around him reflected what he was. Sam could see in his expression hauteur, where before she had seen merely a certain austere withdrawal which she had translated as a sign of a complex and fascinating personality. The hands Vere extended to those who had come to welcome him were covered in the same flesh that had touched her, but the heavy dark emerald ring glowing in the sunlight surely testified to the fact that those hands controlled the lives of others.

There was no place in this man's life for her. The days might have gone when an Eastern ruler installed his women in the seraglio, where no other male eyes could see them and where their days were wasted in an emptiness of waiting to be chosen to share his bed, but Sam suspected her role would be a traditional one nevertheless.

Dressed in her new clothes, she would be expected to live in the shadows, a symbol of her master's wealth and status, a toy for him to play with when the mood took him, to be returned to the shadows to wait for him to want her again.

Vere's gaze searched the small crowd, and came to rest on Sam's pale set face.

He could give instructions now that she was to be put on a plane home and, once he had compensated her financially for the disruption to her life, dismiss her from his thoughts. He could make amends for the loss of her job by ensuring that she was offered more lucrative work elsewhere. There were any number of ways in which he could ensure that he owed her nothing and had no moral obligations towards her. There was no logical reason for him to complicate his life by keeping her here.

No logical reason, no.

He gave a brief nod of his head. Two men stepped forward, bowing to Sam.

Miserably, Sam allowed herself to be guided towards yet another waiting limousine.

This time she was travelling in it alone, whilst Vere rode ahead of her in a different car, with two other men.

The road on which they were travelling was straight and wide. To one side of it lay the sea, a perfect shade of blue-green beneath the late-afternoon sunshine. To the other side lay what Sam presumed must be the city of Dhurahn, and then set aside from it was an area of tall modern glass-fronted skyscrapers, located in what looked like landscaped gardens.

Their route was lined with palm trees set into immaculate flowerbeds with green verges. Through the dark tinted windows of the limousine she could see the people in the vehicles on the other side of the road turning to look at their cavalcade.

Up ahead of them Sam could see a huge wall, in which a pair of wrought-iron gates were opening to allow them through into a courtyard beyond them. The tails of the peacocks shaped in the wrought-iron gates shimmered in the sunlight just as richly as the real thing, the emerald-green of the stones set in them surely the exact shade of Vere's eyes. Vere. She must not think of him as Vere any more. She must think of him instead as the Ruler of Dhurahn. That way maybe she could distance herself properly from him.

A flight of polished cream marble steps led up to a portico, its heavy wooden doors already open and the steps themselves lined with liveried servants.

Vere was already out of his car and striding up the steps.

As she watched him disappear inside the doors, Sam could feel herself starting to panic. She felt lost, abandoned, vulnerable and alone. She also felt angry and resentful because of those feelings.

Someone was opening the car door. Reluctantly Sam got out.

One of the liveried men bowed respectfully. 'If you will come this way, please?'

Silently Sam followed him inside. The large hallway was cool and filled with shadows after the heat outside. Intricately carved shutters blocked the heat of the sunlight from coming through the windows. The marble floor was bare of rugs, and in the middle of it was a raised rectangular pool. The surface of the water was covered in creamy white rose petals. A traditional burning censer stood on one of the steps, giving off a warm spicy scent.

The only furniture in the room was several low divans with gilded legs and armrests, standing against the walls, their silk cushions a splash of colour against the plain white walls. Several sets of inner closed doors opened off the hallway, their dark wood carved with Arabic designs. Coloured glass lamps in fretted ironwork hung from the ceiling, along with several more censers.

'Welcome to Dhurahn, Madam,' said a small dark-haired girl with a soft voice, who seemed to have appeared out of nowhere to bow and gesture across the hallway. 'I am Masiri. If you will allow me, I shall show you to the women's quarters.'

The women's quarters! Sam shivered. But what else could she do but follow Masiri up the long flight of marble stairs and then along a gallery through which the hallway down below could only be seen through a protective fretted screen?

Another flight of stairs and another corridor, this one in the form of an upper veranda that overlooked an enclosed courtyard and garden. Sam caught her breath as she looked down into it, her misery momentarily forgotten as she admired its beauty. A fountain sent droplets of water upwards to sparkle in the sunlight before falling back to dimple the smooth surface of a pool. Large lazy goldfish half hidden by water lily leaves basked in the warmth. The air was full of the scent of the roses planted in the flowerbeds.

'His Highness Prince Vere lives in the old part of the palace, whilst his brother His Highness Prince Drax lives in the new part,' Masiri explained in careful English, adding, 'you are to have the rooms of the Lady Princess. It was for her that her husband built the garden.'

Sam forced a smile and nodded her head, although she had no real idea who Masiri meant.

The girl had stopped outside a pair of double doors, and now opened them.

Reluctantly Sam stepped inside—and then stopped. The room in which she was standing was a beautiful drawing room, decorated as though it were in a classically styled Georgian mansion. It was a woman's room, Sam saw at once, its furniture delicate and feminine—a pretty mahogany writing desk, a pair of matching sofa tables—

and there was even an embroidery screen and a sewing box. A large gilt-framed mirror hung over an Adam-style fireplace; pale green watered silk covered the walls and hung at the windows. A carpet woven in the same pattern and colours as the plasterwork on the ceiling covered the floor.

The whole room was so elegant, its furnishings so obviously antique, that Sam could only gaze at her surroundings in bemusement and awe.

Smiling at her, Masiri led the way to another pair of double doors telling Sam, 'Here is the bedroom for you, madam.'

Dutifully Sam followed her.

The bedroom was decorated in the same style as the drawing room, and in the same colours. The large bed had pale green silk drapes lined in gold silk, and the bedspread was green silk embroidered with gold.

'Here is a dressing room and a bathroom,' Masiri enunciated carefully, indicating the doors on either side of the bed. 'I go now and bring you coffee and some food.'

Sam nodded her head. Her head had started to ache. She walked into the dressing room. Mirrored wardrobes lined one wall, throwing back to her an image of herself that depressed her. They had been travelling virtually all day, and her serviceable long-sleeved khaki shirt and skirt looked dull and dusty—and decidedly un-mistress-like.

She opened one of the wardrobe doors and then stiffened, quickly opening another. There, hanging up neatly, were the clothes Vere had bought. They had obviously been brought to the palace ahead of them and swiftly unpacked.

Another woman might welcome a life in which unseen

hands performed every single necessary task and all one had to do was allow oneself to be waited on, but Sam didn't.

When Masiri returned with coffee and a plate of small sweet pastries, Sam was waiting impatiently for her.

'I want to see His Highness,' she told her determinedly. 'There is something that I need to tell him.'

'You wish His Highness to come to you?' Masiri asked uncertainly.

From the look on Masiri's face Sam suspected that she viewed her request as a breach of protocol, but she didn't care.

'Either he comes to me or you take me to him. It doesn't matter which,' Sam told her firmly. 'But I must see him as soon as possible.'

Vere looked at the note his PA had handed him and read it quickly.

Sam wanted to see him. He looked down at his desk, where his staff had neatly stacked that correspondence they felt Vere would need to see most urgently.

He also should, as a matter of good manners, seek out his sister-in-law and enquire after her health. Drax would expect that of him at the very least. Sadie was a very modern young woman, who was determined to ensure that her husband and her brother-in-law did everything they could to promote sexual equality amongst their own people, and Vere supported her in that. And even if he had not done so, even if there had been issues on which they had clashed, he would have forgiven her them because of the love she had for his twin.

Initially Drax had brought her to Dhurahn as a bride for Vere, not himself, as part of his scheme to prevent them both from being forced into diplomatic marriages. Drax with the Emir's eldest daughter, and Vere with the Ruler of Zuran's youngest sister. Neither of them had welcomed their neighbours' marital plans, but they had agreed that they had to be dealt with tactfully and a plausible reason found for refusal. It had been Drax who had suggested that their best way out of the situation would be for them to provide *themselves* with wives, before either the Ruler or the Emir could broach the subject of formal negotiations.

When Drax had fallen in love with the prospective wife he had chosen for Vere, Vere had been happy for both of them—and happy for himself too. Drax's marriage meant that he could fob off both his neighbours attempts to marry him into their families by pointing out that it was impossible for him to agree without risking offending one of them.

Ultimately he imagined that when he did marry it would be a diplomatic marriage, though one which he chose. The very thought of the vulnerability that falling in love brought made him stiffen his defences against it.

'You will not be able to escape your fate, brother,' Drax had teased him. 'You wait and see. You will follow the same path as our forebears and fall in love with a European woman. It is written into our genes, its course set into the stars. There is no escape.'

Drax was wrong, of course. Totally wrong.

He was, Vere realised, still holding his PA's note, telling him that Sam was asking to see him as a matter of urgency.

Just thinking about her waiting for him set off a reaction

within him that underlined everything he was fighting against. She touched parts of him—his emotions, his self-control… Witness the way he had allowed her to urge his possession of her when he should have withdrawn. Vere could feel the colour crawling up under his skin even though he tried to suppress it. It was no use. He could not withstand the turbulent surge of desire that crashed through him, breaching every defence he tried to put up against it.

Images, scents, sounds filled his head, until his own breathing quickened in time to the remembered race of hers. He moved uncomfortably in his chair, all too aware of the heavy pulse of his erection. If he went to her now he wouldn't be able to trust himself not to touch her. But why *shouldn't* he touch her?

Without telling her the truth? Without giving her the opportunity to judge properly for herself whether or not she still wanted him? His parents would have abhorred such an attitude, and so too did he. If he went to her now… If he went to her now, feeling like this, he was afraid of what he might say and do. Better to wait until he was more in control of himself.

Vere crushed the note and then released it to drop onto his desk, ignoring it to focus on the other papers in front of him.

CHAPTER NINE

IT WAS several hours since the sun had set. His desk was virtually clear, and Vere realised guiltily that he had not been to see Sadie.

It didn't take him long to walk through the old part of the palace and into the new modern wing that Drax had designed.

Sadie smiled when she saw him, offering to send for coffee for him, but Vere shook his head.

'You are well? Drax told me that you have been tired.'

'I am very well,' she assured him. 'And as for me being tired, yes, I was—but now that I am home I feel much better.'

Vere knew that she would have heard about Sam, but she was far too tactful to ask any questions. Unlike his twin.

'Drax is returning immediately the conference ends,' he commented.

'I hope so.'

Vere remained with her for half an hour, but he could see that she was, as Drax had said, looking tired, so he didn't linger.

Now all he had to do was respond to Sam's earlier summons.

He had made up his mind that he must tell her the truth and admit how much he had misjudged and wronged her. It had been easy to set aside his own strong moral scruples when he had believed that at least part of her reason for having sex with him was because she was in the Emir's pay, and therefore he had no responsibility towards her. But now he knew that was not the case, which meant that her desire for him must be genuine.

Whilst his flesh welcomed and indeed embraced that knowledge, his mind wanted to withdraw from it. And his emotions?

Vere cursed himself under his breath as he felt his body respond to the question with its now familiar ache for her.

Sam had waited for Vere for what had felt like hours, and then, when he hadn't appeared, she had showered the grime of the day from her tired body and wrapped herself in a towel, simply intending to sit in the drawing room for a few minutes.

Instead she had fallen asleep in the chair, and that was where Vere found her when he walked into the room.

She was lying with her head against the arm of the chair at an angle that could only result in her waking up with a stiff neck, and her hair looked damp, as though she had fallen asleep without drying it. Her lashes lay against her cheek in soft dark fans. Her lips parted naturally as she breathed, and in the dimly lit room the exposed flesh of her throat and shoulder gleamed with the luminescence of the purest mother-of-pearl.

Vere could feel his heart thudding as heavily as though it had become destabilised, crashing into his ribs with all the recklessness of a man about to haul himself over a precipice, oblivious to his own danger, driven only by a soul-deep need.

She looked so vulnerable and alone. There were smudges beneath her eyes—had she been crying? He could feel the weight of his own guilt.

Somehow he managed to wrench his thoughts back to where they should be. She was just a sleeping woman, that was all.

A sleeping woman whom he had held in his arms in the tranquillity that had followed the intensity of their shared orgasm. He could remember how it had felt to have her burrowing against him, wanting and needing him, finding her security in being with him. Trusting him.

Shame vied inside him with a feeling of almost melancholic sweetness that poured softly through his veins like warmed honey. Now was not the time to disturb her, and possibly distress her with what he had to say. His admissions and her questions could wait until morning. Though he couldn't leave her there to sleep so uncomfortably.

He leaned down, lifting her from the chair, his intention merely to carry her over to the bed and then leave her.

However, he had barely taken more than a couple of steps when she woke up, stiffening, and then relaxing as she said his name with recognition and relief.

She reached out to hold onto him, turning her own body into his. 'I'm so glad you're here.' Her voice was soft with sleep and contentment. Automatically Vere tightened his hold on her.

Sleepily Sam clung to Vere's strength as he carried her into the bedroom and towards the bed. She had been so angry, so determined to tell him that she wanted to leave, but somehow now that he was here, and she was in his arms, that anger had evaporated like the pools of water created overnight by the cold desert air, disappearing in the morning heat of the sun as though they had never been.

She loved him so much. Surely with that love she would be able to show him how much she needed the respect that came from knowing he valued her and cared about her.

He was placing her on the bed. Lovingly she reached up to him, twining her arms round his neck as the towel slipped away from her body, and she breathed out his name against his skin in a soft sound of pleasure.

He must not stay here, Vere warned himself. But as he reached to unclasp her hands from behind his neck Sam pressed her mouth against his in a kiss of sweet command, the tip of her tongue tormenting the closed line of his lips with eager little impatient caresses.

Vere could feel his resolve crumbling to dust—less than dust. It was nothing, gone, forgotten as he let her tease him into submitting to her pleasure. Her tongue slipped between his parted lips, causing Vere to shudder in violent need as it found his and flirted with it, coaxing and cajoling. In the moonlight Vere could see the stiff tightness of her nipples, erect with arousal, and the curve of her breast demanding the cup of his hand around its soft weight. He probed the urgent thrust of her nipple with the pad of his thumb, stroking it, rubbing it erotically, feeling her going wild with sexual excitement. Her tongue meshed with his, submitting to its control of their pleasure. Her hands were trying to push away the fabric that was coming between her and his flesh. She moaned beneath his kiss, her whole body trembling.

He reached out with his free hand to caress the curve of her hip, his own body gripped by unbearable need when she arched upwards, opening her thighs to offer him the gift of her desire for him.

Her sex pulsed with the frantic demand that was throbbing through his own aroused flesh. She was moist and hot, crying out to him when he touched her.

It was more than he could endure.

He undressed quickly and Sam wound her arms around him, pressing her body close to him and kissing every bit of him she could reach…his throat, his shoulder, his chest, and then, to his shock, his belly, making his already hard erection swell and stiffen even more. Abandoning the last of his clothes, Vere picked her up and placed her down on the bed, his mouth against her breast, tightening around her nipple and drawing rhythmically on it whilst Sam gasped and cried out that it was too much pleasure for her to bear.

Her body was already convulsing into the beginning of her orgasm when he entered her, and he felt her flesh tighten on him and possess him, until his cry of release mingled with her own.

'Oh, Vere. I knew right from the start that it would be like this for us.' Sam clung to him emotionally, her voice reflecting the intensity of her experience whilst her heartbeat slowed back down to its normal rate.

How could she not love him and want him to love her after what they had just shared? She felt so bonded with him, so very aware of how much he completed her in ways that no one else ever could. During their lovemaking she had given herself to him, completely and totally. This was how she would want their child to be conceived, in an act of total commitment and giving, so that it would be born carrying that gift of love within its genes.

'Stay with me,' she whispered.

How had it come to this? Vere wondered helplessly as his arms closed round her, holding her to him. This wasn't what he had intended when he had come to her.

Wasn't it? Did he really believe that? Or had he known all along what the outcome would be once he touched her?

Soon Sam had fallen asleep. Vere rested his chin on top of her head. It felt so right, being here with her like this— *she* felt so right. A sensation as though a rock was being lifted away from a guarded, painful place inside him eased gently though him.

'Stay with me,' she had asked him, those words like a tender healing touch on a sore place, overlaying his own painful teenage cry to his parents of, 'Don't leave me'.

Sam woke up abruptly, her hand on the empty space in the bed where Vere should have been. He had gone, left her. The pain inside her was raw and cruel.

She could smell coffee, and the shutters to the French doors had been opened to let in the bright morning light. She pulled on her robe, its long filmy sleeves covering her arms, and stepped through the open doors into the enclosed private courtyard garden.

The sun warmed her skin, and bees hummed busily as they worked. Sam paused to breathe in the scent of a newly opened rose. A shadow fell across the path, and her heart turned over inside her chest in a leap of joy.

'Vere!'

He was showered, his hair still damp, and the smell of soap was on his skin as he came and stood beside her.

'I want to talk to you,' he told her quietly.

Vere had been awake before dawn, lying with Sam's body a sweet weight in his arms, whilst a much heavier and less pleasant weight lay on his conscience.

It had been his own manservant who had discreetly brought fresh coffee and fruit.

'If it's about the clothes—' Sam began, but Vere shook his head

'No, it isn't about the clothes. When we first met in Zuran you had no idea who I was, did you?'

'No, I didn't,' Sam agreed truthfully.

Vere exhaled.

'I know you thought…that is, you suggested…I don't normally…I couldn't help myself,' Sam admitted. 'I looked at you and I knew that my life had changed for ever.'

How could he ever have thought of her as duplicitous? Her honesty shone from her, shaming him.

'I…I felt…something too.'

It astonished Vere that he should make such an admission, but he had been compelled to do so, unable to deny the words that had surely come from his conscience.

'Not that I wanted to.'

'No. I could tell that,' Sam agreed. But something had changed. She could sense it, although she wasn't sure yet what it was. She knew what she was hoping it was. Perhaps miracles could happen? Perhaps Vere could love her? Not just physically desire her.

'Before I left here for your camp we'd been alerted to the fact that someone within the camp was in the pay of the Emir of Khulua. The Emir is our neighbour, and on the surface there is cordiality between us, but he is of the old school and likes nothing better than to create situations which he can work to his advantage. We'd been warned that he was likely to raise questions about the legitimacy of our shared borders. Not because he genuinely believes they are not legitimate. They are. No, what he was looking to do was to put us in a defensive position.'

Sam listened, wondering if his natural concern about such a matter had been responsible for the way he had behaved towards her initially when he had arrived at the camp. Perhaps what she had thought was hostility had merely been anxiety and preoccupation. She could understand that this was a serious matter for him as the Ruler of Dhurahn.

Vere's expression was very grave, and he was speaking slowly, as though he was having to choose his words with great care.

'When I discovered that you had been questioning the course of the Dhurahni river—'

'You were very angry with me?' Sam supplied for him. She shook her head and then reached out to him, placing her hand on his arm. 'I was hurt at the time, because I didn't understand why you were angry. I understand now that you've explained about the Emir, though. Do you know who it is the Emir has been paying?'

Here was the opportunity, the opening he needed. A gut-wrenching pain tore at him. She was being so tender and understanding. She had no idea how little he deserved her concern, or how badly he had maligned her in his own thoughts. But soon she would.

'I believed that I did.' Vere turned away from her. He couldn't bear to look at her when he told her. He didn't want to see the warmth die from her eyes to be replaced by the condemnation he knew he deserved.

Sam could feel the first prickle of an uneasy sense of anxiety, and dread chilled through her body.

Something was wrong. In fact something was very wrong indeed.

'When I saw you on the path by the oasis I didn't want to recognise you. What had happened between us in Zuran wasn't something I wanted to remember—nor was it fitting behaviour for the son my parents would have expected me to be.'

Vere could see the pain in her eyes, and it shocked him to realise how much he wanted to take that pain away from her. He put his hands on her upper arms, struggling not to allow himself to be distracted by the soft smoothness of her skin beneath the sleeves of her robe,

Sam bit into her bottom lip. She was being over-emotional, she knew, but it hurt knowing that he had had such a low opinion of her.

'The truth was that I hadn't forgotten you—because I couldn't. Your memory was embedded in my senses. But I couldn't let it stay there. I needed a reason to make myself resist you. It was no longer enough for me to tell myself that my desire was something I had to control. Out of that need I convinced myself that *you* were the Emir's tool and in his pay.'

Sam's face had lost its colour. She looked every bit as shocked and upset as he had imagined she would. She pulled back from him and he let her go.

'You thought that of me? But you made love to me… you asked me to be your mistress.' Sam was stumbling over the words, trembling as she spoke them, desperately wanting to hear him say that she had misheard him.

'I believed it was my duty to…to get close enough to you to find out what you were doing.'

Sam could feel horror dripping through her, numbing her at first, and then seizing her with a gigantic pain that held her like a vice, allowing her no escape.

'No…' she protested.

She wanted to turn and run, to hide herself from him. But there was no escape. He was speaking again, paralysing her where she stood.

'I decided that the best way to undermine the Emir would be for me to publicly take you, his tool, as my mistress.'

Vere heard her small whimper, like that of a small creature caught in the cruel talons of a hawk.

'I had to put Dhurahn first.'

Sam listened in silence. Was that an explanation or an excuse? she wondered. Did she even care any more? He had hurt her more than she deserved, and certainly more than she could endure. He had used her, knowing she'd believed he wanted her.

From somewhere she summoned the last shreds of her pride to demand, 'Why are you telling me this now?'

'Because whilst we were on our way here my brother rang to say that the investigations I had ordered showed that it wasn't possible for you to be in the Emir's pay. I have wronged you, and for that I can only apologise and beg your forgiveness. Naturally I shall make whatever recompense is needed to ensure that your career does not suffer because of this. As a cartographer—'

'My *career*?' Sam stopped him as she battled against her pain. 'How do you propose to recompense me for my loss of pride and self-respect? For the fact that you let me think you wanted me, and that you—'

She couldn't go on. Tears flooded her eyes, emotion suspending her voice.

Vere went to her.

'No!' She denied him as he made to take her in his arms, beating her fists impotently against his chest in an agony of distraught despair, forcing Vere to let her go.

She had turned away from him, heading back inside the palace, when it happened: a darting movement, liquid and quicksilver, then Sam's shocked cry, the telltale puncture wound in her leg. Then his own reaction as he reached her and told her not to move, knowing what even the slightest action would send the snake's venom speeding fatally towards her heart.

'Keep still and trust me,' he told her, pausing only to call for help before he dropped down on his haunches to take hold of her leg and place his mouth against the puncture marks, desperately trying to suck the poison from them.

Vere's voice had become oddly distorted and echoy, his expression contorted. She tried to move, but his fierce command of, 'No—keep still,' ricocheted through her.

Servants alerted by Vere's cry came hurrying towards them, but even whilst he told them to summon his doctor

Vere didn't take his gaze off Sam, fixing it on her as though by doing so he could fill her with his own strength and somehow keep her alive until she could be given the necessary antidote to the snake's poison.

The gardens were kept rigorously free of snakes, but somehow this one—one of the most poisonous of all—had got in. Vere could feel his heart thudding and pumping with the life force that Sam so badly needed. If he could have opened his veins and given her life he knew he would have done so. She was everything to him. Without her he was nothing, his life an empty wasteland.

Like a desert sandstorm whipped up by the winds of fate the truth stormed through him, refusing to allow him to deny its existence any longer.

He loved her.

Vere's eyes burned with emotion. He couldn't lose her. Not now—not when he loved and needed her so much.

He could feel the beat of Sam's heart slowing down. Her pulse was so weak it was barely there. He would not lose her. He would *not*.

The doctor arrived, his expression grave and taut with concern. In the space of the time it took him to reach into his case for the antidote Sam's lips turned blue.

The doctor put down the hypodermic needle.

'No!' Vere denied fiercely. *'No!'*

'Highness, it is too late.'

The doctor's voice held a finality that Vere could not accept. Images, memories flooded through his heart: the messenger who had brought them the news of their parents' death, the long flight he and Drax had had to make to accompany their bodies back to Dhurahn for their state funeral, the grief and anger that had possessed him ever since. He could not lose Sam as well. He could not. His hand tightened on her wrist, and miraculously he felt a pulse; her chest lifted slightly.

'Look,' he commanded.

Nodding his head, the doctor reached for the syringe.

CHAPTER TEN

SAM put down the book she had been trying to read. She was sitting in the elegant drawing room that Vere had told her had been decorated for his great-grandmother. She had eaten her solitary dinner, and now she looked at her watch.

Vere had been so loving and tender towards her whilst she had been recovering, coming to talk to her often and letting her know that it was her colleague James who had been the Emir's pay. But now that she had been pronounced fully well and allowed to get up out of bed he had retreated into a coldness that left her feeling desperately hurt and confused. She hadn't seen him at all today, apart from one brief visit during which he had made no attempt to hold her or even talk properly to her. His voice had been sharp and somehow almost hostile.

She was beginning to feel that she must have imagined that moment when she had opened her eyes to find him sitting at her bedside, had thought she had heard him whispering to her that he loved her and feared to lose her. She must have done, because he certainly wasn't behaving as though he loved her now. She suspected that she regretted having spoken such words to her. But why? He must know that she loved *him*. After all, she hadn't made any attempt to hide her feelings from him.

Was it really only a little over twenty-four hours since he had sat with her in the darkness of her room, holding her hand and cupping her face in his hands, whispering emotionally how much she meant to him?

'I can't wait for Dr Sayid to pronounce you fully fit. My bed has been as empty without you as my heart and my life would be if I lost you. I yearn to be with you, flesh to flesh, heart to heart and mind to mind. With nothing between us, no barriers to separate us.'

Sam's heart turned over now, just replaying those words inside her head. Vere was such a passionate lover. Going into his arms was like opening a door into their own secret special world.

And yet now that Dr Sayid had pronounced her properly well, instead of taking her to his bed, as she so longed for him to do, Vere was ignoring her.

Why?

She ought to try and find out, Sam knew, but she just didn't think she had the courage—even though a part of her said that she should find it. By staying here without knowing the truth of what Vere's feelings were she was cheating them both, not just herself. Vere needed to be free to share his life with a woman he loved, and she was not that woman.

Her close brush with death had changed her, Sam recognised, making her all too aware of her physical vulnerability and the uncertainty of life, but at the same time giving her new emotional strength and an unshakable belief in the importance and value of love.

Like life itself, true love should not be treated lightly nor taken for granted. It demanded respect and the most tender of care.

She had had plenty of time to think about his life and the role she could reasonably expect to play in it whilst she had been recovering from the snake bite, and now that she was over the initial shock of his revelations about his mis-judgement of her she was desperately trying to see past them and focus instead on the care he had shown her whilst she was ill. A care, she comforted herself, which must indicate that she meant *something* to him.

Vere stood in front of the formal state portrait of his parents. It dominated the palace's formal audience room. It was here that subjects traditionally came to speak to their Ruler, and to have their voices heard.

The portrait was extraordinarily lifelike. During the early months after their death Vere had often come here to look at it, almost as though by focusing on the couple it would somehow bring them back to life. But of course he had known that this was not possible, and he had always left the room feeling as though he couldn't bear the weight of his own pain.

It was in this room, beneath this portrait, that he had made a solemn mental vow that he must separate himself from his own vulnerability for the sake of his people, and that he must never allow himself to fall in love.

How could he rule wisely and properly if he was con-stantly in fear of life taking from him the person he loved? He could not.

But he had broken that vow in loving Sam, hadn't he?

Vere knew he would never forget how he had felt when he had thought she was dying. He had had a vision then of his own future, his life stretching out ahead of him as a barren wasteland of nothingness.

But he could not afford that kind of vulnerability. Like someone once burned, he was mortally afraid of the remembered pain and of suffering it again. Better to live without the warmth of fire than to risk the agony it could inflict.

He couldn't keep Sam here now. He knew that. It was too dangerous.

A protective veil had been ripped away from inside his heart, allowing him to see what was hidden inside it. He couldn't pretend to himself any longer that it was only physical desire he felt for her, and that it was therefore safe to keep her with him in his life and in his bed.

He couldn't send her away yet, though. Not until he was one hundred percent sure that she was fully recovered. It was all very well for Dr Sayid to say that she was, but Vere suspected that she still wasn't restored to full physical strength. And besides, where would she go? How would she support herself?

A surge of protective urgency so strong that it caught him off-guard thundered through him. He looked up at his parents' portrait. His father's arm rested protectively around his mother. The gesture reflected just how he wanted to keep Sam within the protection of his own love. But who could protect him from the pain he would suffer if he should lose her for any reason?

The only person who could do that was himself, by not loving her in the first place.

CHAPTER ELEVEN

IT WAS two days now since Sam had been told she was fully recovered, but she hadn't seen Vere even once during that time... Tears pricked at Sam's eyes. She felt abandoned and rejected, not knowing what she had done to cause Vere to treat her in such a way.

She put down the book she had been pretending to read and got up to wander aimlessly round the room, relieved to have someone else to talk to when Masiri appeared with a tray of coffee.

'I am sorry I am late,' she apologised. 'Only the Princess called me and I had to go...'

'The Princess?' Sam queried uncertainly.

Vere had made no mention of any princess living in the palace.

'Yes.' Masiri nodded her head vigorously. 'The Princess. She is the wife of His Highness. She has been away, visiting her own country, but now she has returned.'

Sam's whole body had gone icy cold with shock.

Vere was *married*?

'The Princess is the Prince's wife?' Sam could hear

herself stammering, as the answer to her question as to why Vere was ignoring her became all too apparent.

'Yes,' Masiri confirmed.

Why hadn't Vere told her he was married?

Did she really need to ask herself that?

He hadn't told her because she was just his lover, his mistress, and men—especially men like Vere—did not discuss their wives with the women they chose to sleep with outside their marriage.

But Vere had told her he loved her.

That was what men told their lovers. And now that his wife was back he was regretting having said those words to her and wanted to back off from her. She hadn't even really been his mistress, had she, never mind had his love? After all, the real reason he had brought her here had nothing to do with him wanting her.

It was as though two separate people were arguing inside her head. One the shamed, betrayed woman deeply in love, the other her cynical bitterly angry counterpart, savage with fury at the part she had unwittingly been forced to play in another woman's marriage.

'The Princess…?'

Masiri was looking at her, waiting for her to continue, but Sam knew that she had no right to ask the questions burning her heart.

'It doesn't matter,' she told Masiri tonelessly.

Vere was married. Another woman had the right to call herself his wife, to share his life and his bed. Another woman. Never in the wildest reaches of her imagination had Sam ever envisaged herself playing the role of 'the other woman'. If she had known right from the start that

Vere was married...if he had told her...then she would never have...

She would never have *what*? Fallen in love with him? Gone to bed with him? Accepted his protection as her lover? At which one did she draw the line?

Sam felt sick with horror and shame.

She couldn't stay here now. She would have to leave. It nauseated her to think what she had done. And what about Vere? How could he have done such a thing? Or did he expect his wife to understand that he had taken Sam to bed for the sake of Dhurahn, and that because of that it didn't mean anything? Would *she* be able to accept that if she had been his wife? Or would it haunt her for the rest of her days that her husband might be lying to her and might have wanted that other woman?

The man she had thought Vere was could never have behaved as Vere had.

His behaviour was unforgivable, and he had dragged her down into its nastiness with him.

Sam knew that she would have left there and then but for the fact that Vere had taken charge of her passport for sakekeeping. She would have to wait until she could see him.

The smell of the coffee Masiri had poured for her before leaving the room was making her feel suffocated and sick. She badly needed some fresh air. She half ran and half stumbled into the pretty courtyard garden, now thankfully free of snakes.

She skirted the fish pond, hurrying down the path that led past it, unable to bear looking at it. Then she noticed for the first time that, almost obscured by the roses that smothered it, there was a high wrought-iron gate in the far wall of the garden.

What lay beyond it? Sam wondered absently, automatically going to look, pleased with any distraction from her thoughts on the horror of the reality of her situation.

At first all she could see was another garden, more modern in concept than the one she was in, ornamented with sleek pieces of artwork in stone and metal set in beds of gravel planted with grasses and spiky plants. Water jetted upwards in a thin straight plume from some unseen source. As she turned away she saw Vere, coming from the far corner of the garden. She drew in her breath. He was dressed in European clothes—a business suit that emphasised the breadth of his shoulders—and the greenery surrounding him threw shadows across his face. Sam waited for her heart to give its normal eager kick of recognition and joy, but strangely it didn't.

He was turning his head away from her, without having seen her, holding out his hand to someone.

A woman came slowly towards him, wearing a white dress, a hat covering her head. She was very obviously pregnant, leaning into him and then smiling up at him. He was putting his arm around her to support her, bending his head to kiss her on the forehead, his hand resting protectively on her swollen body.

The desire to be violently sick cramped Sam's insides. Unable to watch any longer, she turned and ran.

Sam had no idea how long she had been sitting there in the garden. She knew that every now and again her body shuddered violently of its own accord, and that in between those shudders her forehead broke out into a sweat. She knew too that she felt slightly light-headed. Light-headed, but oh, so very heavy-hearted.

Was Vere still with his wife? Was he cradling her and their child, his hand resting on the womanly flesh that held the new life they had created together, as it had done when she had seen them in the garden? Her teeth started to chatter together, but it was far from cold.

She could hear light footsteps on the path. Masiri, no doubt, coming to see where she was and if she wanted more coffee.

She stood up clumsily, the colour leaving her face as she stepped forward and saw that it wasn't Masiri but Vere's wife.

'Oh, I'm sorry—I've startled you and I didn't mean to.'

She had a light musical voice, and her smile was warm and genuine. 'I've seen you walking in the garden, and I've been dying to come and talk to you. You're English as well, aren't you?'

Sam nodded her head, completely unable to speak.

'I shouldn't really be doing this, of course.' She laughed, a soft, indulgent sound. 'Vere won't approve at all, and will be cross with me, I know, but I was so curious about you I couldn't resist.'

Sam fought to match her calm, easy manner, feeling as though she had strayed into some surreal and alien world

'Yes. Yes, you must have been curious.'

'I can't stay very long.' She patted her stomach and pulled a face. 'Vere's been worrying that I might go into labour before my due date. I'm Sadie, by the way. I do hope that we're going to be friends.'

Friends!

'Yes,' Sam agreed, wondering inwardly what on earth she was saying. She could never, ever be a friend to Vere's wife. This was tearing her apart, destroying her. How could his wife be so nice to her? Unless…maybe she didn't know that Vere had made love to her? Yes, that must be it, Sam decided feverishly. She didn't know. Vere must have lied to her. How could it hurt so much, loving a man she knew wasn't worthy of that love?

'I'd better go,' Sadie was saying. 'I don't want Vere to come and catch me here with you.'

Sam could feel herself trembling violently as she watched Sadie walk back the way she had come.

She had to get away from here. If only she could access her passport, Sam thought. She would do anything to escape her searing pain and equally searing guilt about having slept with Sadie's husband. She didn't have anything much to pack, as she certainly didn't intend to take with her the clothes Vere had bought for her, even if she had given in and worn them these last few days.

Where was Vere now? With his wife? Reassuring her that she and their child were all that mattered to him? Was he whispering to Sadie the words of love and passion he had whispered to her? She would have to go and see him to demand that he return her passport, but she didn't have any fears now that he would try to prevent her from leaving. He would probably be all too relieved to see her go.

Sam went back to her room and asked Masiri to have a message sent to Vere, telling him that she had to see him urgently.

* * *

Vere had been on the point of getting together with his twin so that Drax could update him on his recent trip when he was informed of Sam's wish to see him 'urgently'.

Sam's use of the word 'urgently' produced within him a dangerous mix of volatile emotions, dominated by a recklessly urgent need of his own that had very little to do with dry dialogue and everything to do with a very male possessive instinct.

He had to confront his vulnerability, Vere decided. Avoiding any kind of contact with Sam was a coward's way of dealing with the situation. A coward who was too weak to send her away, not strong enough to trust his own self-control. He inclined his head and gave instructions for Sam to be brought to his office.

The fact that Vere was seeing her in his office told her everything she needed to know, thought Sam as she was bowed into it, to find Vere seated at his desk, apparently engrossed in reading some documents he had in front of him.

He couldn't have made it more obvious that it was over between them, and of course Sam knew exactly why. Beneath her pain the volcano of her pride sent up a lava-hot surge of protective anger.

'It's all right Vere,' she told him. 'I haven't come to beg you to take me to bed, or to remind you about what you said to me when I was ill.'

Sam had the satisfaction of seeing the way the muscle in his jaw tensed beneath the lash of her latter comment.

'All I want is my passport.'

He was looking at her now, a flicker of something unreadable briefly darkening his eyes before he averted his gaze.

'So silly of me to feel concerned that I might be burdening you with my unwanted love, and *that* is why you haven't been anywhere near me for the last couple of days, when the real reason is that your wife has returned to the palace. And so very naïve of me not to have guessed that you were married.'

She loved him. But then of course he knew that, because he now knew her. He knew that without loving a man she could not and would not give herself in the way she had given herself to him.

A pain, slow and sharp and unending, was piercing him. He must endure it, because it was the price he had to pay for his future without her, and for the emotional security that future without Sam would bring him.

'Your wife—*Sadie*—came to see me.' Sam gave a laugh that was too high-pitched and haunted with despair. 'She seemed to like me. She said she wanted us to be friends.'

All Vere had to do to stop her pain was tell her that she'd got it wrong and that Sadie was Drax's wife. All he had to do to stop his own pain was take her in his arms and tell her that *she* was the one he loved, the one he would always love.

All he had to do to cross the chasm that separated his past from a future filled with love was to push his way past that mental imagine of his mother's body, her face frozen into an unnatural calm by the undertaker's skill. It had been his duty to see her—a horror from which he had protected Drax by taking it upon his shoulders alone.

Only he knew how often during those hours it had been touch and go for Sam. He had seen that memory reform inside his head, with Sam's face replacing his mother's. A fierce shudder ripped through him.

No wonder he shivered at the thought of his wife befriending her, thought Sam bitterly.

'I'm packed and ready to leave, so if you will give me my passport I'm sure you'll be only too happy to see that I get the first empty seat on a plane leaving for Zuran.' Her head lifted proudly as she spoke. Not for the world was she going to let him see the heartache she was feeling inside.

It was the perfect solution to a situation that had become untenable and, if he was honest, unbearable. Far better to let Sam think the worst of him, for her to walk away from him despising and hating him—for her sake. Perhaps, in fact, that was the best gift he could give her. He had no idea just how she had come to think that Sadie was his wife, but it made sense to let her go on thinking so.

He opened one of the drawers in his desk and removed her passport, placing it down on the desk between them and then withdrawing from it.

Sam could almost taste her own bitterness. He obviously didn't even want to risk touching her fingers.

How could she still care, knowing as she did what kind of cheat he was?

Where was her self-respect? Crushed, like her dreams, beneath the weight of her heavy heart.

Vere pressed the buzzer that would summon one of his aides, telling him when he arrived to organise a car to take Sam to the airport.

'By the time you reach the airport a flight will have been

arranged for you.' Even if that meant sending her out of Dhurahn in the royal jet, Vere decided, as he started to stand up. 'My brother is waiting to see me, so if you will excuse me I will leave my PA to escort you to your car.'

It was over, thought Sam shakily. Over? How could it ever be over when she still loved him? her heart protested. But she could not listen to it, because if she did she would surely shame herself utterly and completely by going to him, clinging to him, begging him… It *was* over. It had to be.

Somehow Sam managed to follow the aide, who was already leaving the room.

She was leaving—just as he had wanted her to do. Now there would be no risk, no struggle between the two opposing forces within him. In severing the link between them he had severed himself—freed himself from a lifetime of fear that she might ultimately abandon him.

He was glad she had gone. From his office window he could see her, getting into the waiting car. She was hesitating, looking over her shoulder and then up towards where he was. Immediately Vere stepped back from the glass.

He must go and see Drax. They had important matters to discuss—matters that involved Dhurahn and its future, matters which he as its Ruler needed to give his full attention to.

The car would have left the palace now, and would be travelling down the Royal Highway. It wasn't very far to the airport, and the plane that would take Sam to Zuran had been delayed to wait for her. And then she would be gone—for ever.

'No!'

The tortured sound of his own denial was thrown back to him by the walls of his office. Vere reached for the telephone.

CHAPTER TWELVE

THEY HAD ALMOST reached the airport. Soon she would be gone from Dhurahn, never to return.

The driver brought the car to an abrupt halt and then did a U-turn, and before Sam could so much as knock on the privacy screen separating them they were speeding back the way they had just come.

Back in the palace courtyard, a servant sprang to open the car door for her. Two aides were waiting to escort her swiftly inside—aides or jailers? Sam wondered apprehensively as they walked either side of her, down now familiar corridors, taking her, she realised, to Vere's private quarters.

Outside the double doors they stopped and knocked, and then opened them for her.

She didn't want to go through them, but somehow she discovered that she had.

Behind her the doors were closed, and she was left confronting Vere.

'Why have you done this?' she demanded.

Her heart was thudding and thundering out of beat, and the loud, out-of-control thump was surely totally betraying her.

'Because I had to,' said Vere.

She had never seen him looking like this before, his emotions clearly revealed in his expression—so clearly that Sam felt as though he was willing her to look at him and see what was there.

She shouldn't be here with him. It was far too dangerous. She took a step backwards, but it was too late; she had hesitated for too long. And now she was in Vere's arms, and he was kissing her with a raw passion more intimate than anything he had shown her before.

Sam knew she should resist and object, but shockingly she was winding her arms round his neck, pressing her body into his and giving herself up to his kiss.

'I couldn't let you go.'

The words, thick, unsteady and wholly honest, tore at her heart.

Such simple words to elicit so many complex feelings. Simple words that were very dangerous. Words that were forbidden between them.

Tears filled Sam's eyes.

'You shouldn't have done this. It's wrong.'

'I love you,' Vere told her fiercely, ignoring her protest.

'You can't. You mustn't.'

It was his own words given back to him. How easy it was now to dismiss them as foolish shadows with no base in reality. Just like his own adolescent fears.

'You have a wife and...soon you will have a child...' A child. What about her own secret? The one that had begun so recently as a joyous hope and had now become a guilty fear—because her baby, if there was to be one, would never know its father or receive his love.

'No. Sadie is not my wife, Sam. She is married to my brother Drax.'

Sam's head swam with the enormity of the message those simple words carried.

'That can't be true.'

'It is true,' Vere insisted. 'And if you won't believe me then I shall ask Drax and Sadie to tell you themselves.'

He meant what he was saying. Sam could see that.

'If you aren't married, then why did you let me think that you were?'

Sam couldn't keep the pain out of her voice and, hearing it, Vere ache with guilt, and with his own desire to hold her and assure her that he would never hurt her again. How best could he explain to her the complexity of the turmoil he had experienced since meeting her?

Whilst he hesitated Sam broke the silence, her voice hesitant and heavy with sadness. 'I love you Vere,' she told him quietly. 'You know that, I know. But I can't... I'm not emotionally equipped to be in a relationship with someone who blows hot one moment and cold the next.'

And more importantly, she could not and would not take that risk for their child—although of course she wasn't going to tell him that. Just as she wasn't going to tell him of her growing suspicions that she might be pregnant.

Shakily she continued, 'I accept that originally you believed you had good reason to be suspicious of me, and that because of that there were times when you backed off from me. But afterwards, once you knew the truth...'

Would she understand if he told her his truth? Would she love him enough to accept his vulnerability and understand it? He had to take the risk and tell her, Vere knew.

He had to make that pledge, give that trust—to her and to their future. Vere wanted so badly to touch her and hold her, but he dared not, because he knew that if he did he would never be able to let her go.

Instead he exhaled and began, 'Your presence was a reminder of…something I didn't want to admit.'

'What something?' Sam asked him. Her mouth had gone dry and her heart was pounding unsteadily and uncomfortably.

'My…my vulnerability.'

Vere's voice was terse.

He had never been able to talk about how it had felt to lose his parents, but his conscience was forcing him to acknowledge that he owed Sam at least some kind of honesty. And besides…to his own surprise he discovered that a part of him actually wanted to tell her.

'Drax and I were in our early teens when our parents were killed in an accident. We were a very close family. My parents were very much in love with one another. To lose them so unexpectedly and in such a way was a terrible shock, but we were their sons—our father's heirs. We had a duty to our people and our country that had to come before our grief.'

His pain was tearing at Sam's heart.

He made a helpless gesture with his hand.

'It is so hard to say or explain. We had our duty, but we had our own feelings as well. For me there was…there was fear and anger as well as loss. We had loved them so dearly. Our mother especially… She was…very loving…very warm. We were of that age when we were just beginning to think ourselves too old to be her "boys" any more, and yet at the same time inside we still needed her comfort. When it was taken from us… The pain of such a loss goes very deep. I… For me it was easier to shut myself off from the risk of it happening again. This isn't easy for me to say, Sam, and I know it won't be easy for you to hear, but there are things I have to tell you that need to be said, so please bear with me?'

Her throat tight with anxiety, Sam nodded her head.

'I didn't want to love you,' Vere admitted. 'In fact I fought every way I knew not to. At first I thought it would be enough for me to simply deny my feelings and to rename them lust.'

Sam winced.

'But then after your snake bite, when you were so close to death, that fabrication was ripped from me. All that mattered to me was that you lived, and that you didn't leave me. But even that was not enough to keep me from my path to self-destruction. Even though I knew that I loved you, and I couldn't deny those feelings any longer, I still fought against giving in—as I saw it—to that love.'

'Why?' Sam challenged him.

When he didn't reply, she made her own assumption and said bleakly, 'I suppose it was because you felt I wasn't the right person for…for a Ruler?'

'No,' Vere assured her swiftly, and truthfully. 'You must never think that. I knew you were the right person for me, and for Dhurahn. I knew you were the perfect person for me, Sam, in fact the only person for me. That was why I fought so hard against loving you. The truth is that the reason I believed I didn't dare allow myself to love you lies in my past and in the death of my parents. I was a young adolescent, just at that stage of being torn between a desire for manhood and a fear of how swiftly I was moving towards it—especially in view of the fact that my father was preparing me for the responsibilities of rulership.

'My mother understood this. She was the only person I felt able to admit my feelings to. As the eldest son and the elder brother I felt I had a duty to be strong. I knew my father loved me, but as with most boys of that age I felt a need to match him emotionally, man to man, and that meant not allowing him to see that I sometimes felt vulnerable and fearful of the future. Of course I realise now that he would have known this, having no doubt come through the same experience himself—and that that, in fact, was why he was trying to prepare me.

'There can never be a good time to lose one's parents, and to say that I simply wasn't prepared to lose mine when I did, that I didn't have the resources in place within me to cope, would be an understatement. The loss of my mother in particular left me feeling abandoned and vulnerable. My feelings overwhelmed and frightened me. But I was Dhurahn's Ruler. I had to be tough.'

Sam made a small sound of loving compassion and told him, 'You were a boy…'

'I was Dhurahn's new Ruler,' Vere corrected her gently.

Sam's tender heart ached with sadness for him.

'The only way I could cope was to tell myself that what I was going through was the worst it could ever be—the worst it would ever be. Because I would never allow myself to be so vulnerable again. I told myself that I must never love someone so much that losing them could affect me so deeply and painfully.

'What happened between us in that hotel corridor in

Zuran breached defences I had believed were inde-
structible. I told myself to ignore what I had felt and simply
pretend that it and you did not exist. But the memory of
you kept me awake at night, tormenting and mocking me.
I told myself what I felt was merely physical attraction, and
I despised myself for wanting you. It was a relief and an
escape route to be able to tell myself that you had an
ulterior motive, and that I must therefore despise you and
be suspicious of you. But love has a mind and an instinct
of its own. Something no doubt my mother would have
told me, if she had lived long enough to guide me through
the treacherous currents of adolescence. My love wasn't
so easily dismissed or forced into accepting convenient
lies.

'I was perched on top of a landslide that would sweep
away all my false beliefs, and that is exactly what did
happen when you were bitten. The thought of losing you
demolished all my defences. I was forced to admit that I
loved you.'

'But as soon as I was well again you backed off from
me.'

'Shedding the protective skin one has worn for so many
years isn't easy or painfree. Doubts flooded into the space
left by my destroyed defences. Yes, I loved you—but that
did not mean that you would never leave me. My old fear
was still there, and if I'm honest perhaps a part of it will
always remain. But what I do know now is that I would
rather live with that fear than without you. That is if you
can bring yourself to love and marry a man who is so very
unworthy of you.'

'You want to marry me?'

'I want to commit to you in every way there is,' Vere said softly.

'When you came to me and told me you wanted to leave I told myself that your going was the best thing that could happen to me. But the minute I visualised you getting on board that plane and leaving me for good I knew that in truth it was the worst, that my life would be meaningless without you. You are my joy, Sam, not my fear. You are my future and not my past.'

'I couldn't stay, thinking you were married,' she whispered to him. 'Not when I loved you so much myself, and not when I wanted your child so desperately.'

Sam looked up at him. He had moved closer, so that their bodies were only a breath apart.

Dared she tell him what she had feared she must keep to herself?

Sam swallowed painfully.

If they were to have a future together then it had to be built on trust and honesty.

'And, most of all, not when I thought that maybe you had already given me that child,' she told him simply.

Vere's reaction was everything she could have hoped for and more. He reached for her, holding her protectively, his eyes brilliant with emotion.

'You are carrying our child?'

'I think so, and I hope so—although it is too early to be sure.'

'My love!' His voice was hoarse with emotion.

'Oh, Vere.'

She loved him so much. But right now Sam knew that her greatest need was to comfort the boy he had been, to take the hand of the man he had become and help him walk free of the shadows of the past into the healing light of the sun.

She went to him and gripped his arms, raising herself up on her toes to kiss him gently, in commitment and in love.

'You are mine. And I warn you that I shall never let you go,' Vere whispered against her lips, before taking the initiative from her and kissing her so intimately that her own passionate response to him left her clinging weakly to him. 'We belong together, you and I, Sam.'

'That's what I felt the first time we met,' Sam told him emotionally. 'And now we are together, and we always will be.'

'Always,' Vere agreed firmly, knowing that it was the truth, and that he could trust in it and in her.

The journey to self-acceptance that he had begun so long ago was now finally completed.

MILLS & BOON

MODERN™

On sale 4th July 2008

BOUGHT FOR REVENGE, BEDDED FOR PLEASURE
by Emma Darcy

Black sheep Jack Maguire has a bargain to make with Sally. She can keep her beloved house, and receive a generous allowance…if she will be his mistress at weekends!

FORBIDDEN: THE BILLIONAIRE'S VIRGIN PRINCESS
by Lucy Monroe

Sebastian Hawk is a billion-dollar master – in business and in the bedroom. Lina is a princess whose provocative innocence makes Sebastian lose his legendary self-control…

THE GREEK TYCOON'S CONVENIENT WIFE
by Sharon Kendrick

Alice is captivated by multi-billionaire Kyros Pavlidis – but he wants a new wife in his bed for reasons that have everything to do with necessity and nothing to do with love…

THE MARCIANO LOVE-CHILD
by Melanie Milburne

Alessandro Marciano has a proposition for Scarlett: he'll bankrupt her or bed her. The choice is hers. But when Alessandro is faced with the fact that Scarlett's child is his son – then there isn't a choice at all…

MILLS & BOON

MODERN

On sale 4th July 2008

THE MILLIONAIRE'S REBELLIOUS MISTRESS

by Catherine George

Alex Merrick is rich and handsome, but to Sarah Carver he's her worst enemy. When Sarah gets the chance to take revenge, the glory doesn't last long – because Alex has an ace up his sleeve...

THE MEDITERRANEAN BILLIONAIRE'S BLACKMAIL BARGAIN

by Abby Green

Cynical, ruthless Dante D'Aquanni is a powerful man with a reputation to uphold. When Alicia Parker turns up at his villa with the press in tow, he's furious! Dante will demand more than just a mere apology...

MISTRESS AGAINST HER WILL

by Lee Wilkinson

Zane Lorenson knows seducing his pretty personal assistant might teach her a lesson... Inexperienced Abigail has adored the dashing billionaire from afar for ages, and she's helpless to resist...

HER RUTHLESS ITALIAN BOSS

by Christina Hollis

Luca Francesco has one condition for Beth Woodbury: she'll assist him by day and warm his bed by night, with no talk of marriage or babies. But soon Beth is pregnant – with her formidable boss's heir!

Available at WHSmith, Tesco, ASDA, and all good bookshops

www.millsandboon.co.uk

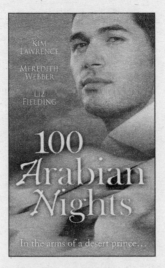
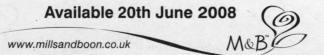

Queens of Romance

Queens of Romance
International Bestselling Authors

PENNY JORDAN
Jet Set Wives

Bedding His Virgin Mistress

Ricardo Salvatore planned to take over Carly's company, so
why not have her as well? But Ricardo was stunned when in
the heat of passion he learned of Carly's innocence…

Expecting the Playboy's Heir

American billionaire and heir to an earldom, Silas Carter is
one of the world's most eligible men. Beautiful Julia Fellowes
is perfect wife material. And she's pregnant!

Blackmailing the Society Bride

When millionaire banker Marcus Canning decides it's time
to get an heir, debt-ridden Lucy becomes a convenient wife.
Their sexual chemistry is purely a bonus…

Available 5th September 2008

Collect all 10 superb books in the collection!

M&B

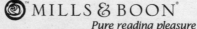

FREE!
4 Books
and a surprise gift!

We would like to take this opportunity to thank you for reading this Mills & Boon® book by offering you the chance to take FOUR more specially selected titles from the Modern™ series absolutely FREE! We're also making this offer to introduce you to the benefits of the Mills & Boon® Reader Service™—

- ★ **FREE home delivery**
- ★ **FREE gifts and competitions**
- ★ **FREE monthly Newsletter**
- ★ **Exclusive Reader Service offers**
- ★ **Books available before they're in the shops**

Accepting these FREE books and gift places you under no obligation to buy, you may cancel at any time, even after receiving your free shipment. Simply complete your details below and return the entire page to the address below. You don't even need a stamp!

YES! Please send me 4 free Modern books and a surprise gift. I understand that unless you hear from me, I will receive 6 superb new titles every month for just £2.99 each, postage and packing free. I am under no obligation to purchase any books and may cancel my subscription at any time. The free books and gift will be mine to keep in any case.

P8ZEF

Ms/Mrs/Miss/Mr .... Initials ....
                                                    BLOCK CAPITALS PLEASE
Surname ....
Address ....

....

.... Postcode ....

Send this whole page to:
UK: FREEPOST CN81, Croydon, CR9 3WZ